Dedicated to my dad, who always believed in me.

CHRISTOPHER J. VALIN

ACKNOWLEDGMENTS

I want to thank everyone who helped make this book possible, starting with my parents, who always encouraged me to do what I loved. I could never have done it without some fellow writers who provided some great feedback, such as my old friends Bret Bernal and Brian DeLay (and Brian's son, Noah); my "inner circle" partners Mike Ezell, Danny Grossman, and Steve Barr; my G10 compatriots, Eugene Ramos, DG McMurry, Chris Whigham, Steve Boudreault, and Sean Marks; my online friend, Harry Connolly for all of his advice; and Mike Leins; also, my current and former co-workers, Adam Bosler, Steve Hall, Russ Reabold, and Alex Nedelkow. And, most of all, I want to thank my wife, Cecille, my daughter, Saylor, and my son, Sawyer, for having to endure long periods without me being present (either in the room or, on occasion, just mentally) while I work on projects such as this one.

ONE

Superhero.

It actually sounds pretty stupid when you say it out loud. Is it one word or two? Hyphenated maybe? Not sure. Most of us masked crime fighters don't use the term.

It also suggests someone has super powers. Me, not so much. I have a really useful ability, but I wouldn't call it a super power. It's kind of like an eidetic memory, only better. Most people would say it's a photographic memory, but that's wrong. I not only remember things, I can copy them. Perfectly.

Because of this, I can learn things really fast. Like martial arts skills. For example, at the moment I'm fighting, like, a dozen gangbangers——make that thirteen, I just noticed the one sneaking up behind me——in a dark alley downtown. But they're making the usual mistake of trying to take me on one or two at a time.

And, as usual, I'm kicking all their asses.

Don't get me wrong: I've trained hard. Really, really hard. Enough to be a black belt in a bunch of different disciplines. But I basically just have to watch a Jackie Chan or Bruce Lee movie——or, better yet, an MMA or UFC match—— and I can imitate every move perfectly.

That's why I'm able to elbow the guy sneaking up behind me in the eye without even looking. You think eyes are off limits? Did you miss the part where I said I was fighting thirteen guys?

And I'm only fifteen. For six and a half more minutes, anyway. At 10:34 p.m. I'll officially hit the big one-six. Yay. *Happy birthday to me.*

You'd think these losers would get the hint after I defeat five or six of them, no problem. I mean, the girl they were trying to assault is long gone now. But no, they keep coming at me, one after another. And even when they do land a punch, the armored parts of my costume—including my helmet—make it so they hurt their hands more than they do me.

I can never understand what these guys are thinking. *I know he just took down five of my buddies without breaking a sweat, but I'm the one who's gonna beat his ass.*

As I take these guys on, I do start to wonder why this seems to be happening so much more lately. Of course, there's always crime in this city, but the past couple of weeks it's starting to get out of control. And not just a little bit. It didn't even build up over time. Just all of a sudden, my job was ten times harder than usual.

Well, not really that hard. It just takes me ten times as long to take care of it.

Punch to the solar plexus. Kick to the jaw. Two more down, and they keep on coming. Then the part that always seems to happen in these situations: The biggest, toughest guy they have steps up and the rest back away. I'm not sure why he's been hanging back, but I have a feeling he wanted the rest to wear me down so he can take me out easier and boost his reputation as a badass.

I'm going to show him just how wrong he is.

He runs at me with a roar and his fist pulled back above his head. This guy obviously never had to learn to fight because he's so big and strong. I barely have to move to step out of his way and watch him plow into the wall behind me.

Now he's really pissed off. And pretty dazed. After shaking his head like a dog just out of the water, he turns and tries to grab me. He probably wants to take me down to the ground so I can't dodge him. I give him a knee to the junk— nope, that's not off limits either. In fact, there's only one rule: *No killing.*

He slumps to his knees, holding his crotch, then falls over on his puckered face like a tree being cut down.

Now the three baddies who are still conscious look at each other and try to escape. I grab two of them and slam their heads together and they fall to the ground.

The third tries to limp away, and even though I'm barely breathing hard, I don't feel like chasing him. I toss my boomerang and tag him at the base of his skull, which may not have knocked him out. But when his face hits the dumpster on his way down, I'm pretty sure he's done with.

That's when I hear *him.*

"Not bad." I hate that gravelly-voice thing he does when he's in costume. I've told him how lame it sounds, but he still insists on it, even when nobody's around to hear it except me.

"Not bad? I thought it was pretty damn good."

He steps out of the shadows, where he's apparently been standing, watching me. With the almost all-black costume, it really isn't that hard for him to do. Unlike me, with my bright-red uniform and blond hair.

"Language."

So ridiculous. He has no problem taking me into situations where I'm more likely than not to get killed or maimed, but I'm not supposed to swear around him.

"Yeah, sorry. How long were you standing there?"

"Long enough." I'm serious, he sounds totally fake. I almost want to laugh sometimes.

"And you didn't think it might be a good idea to, I don't know, give me a hand?"

"You didn't need any help." Wow. From The Black Harrier, that's pretty much the highest compliment you can get. "But there are still some things we need to work on to increase your efficiency."

I nod and decide not to ask him where he was all night, even though it's the fifth time in a couple of weeks I've had to patrol alone.

"Is tomorrow okay?" I always have to confirm things with him. Never assume.

"Tomorrow."

"Okay, then. Well, I think I'm pretty much done here. Sounds like the cops are on the way. I need to get home to finish my homework and check on my mom."

He grunts. He always gets extra-broody when I bring up my mom. I swear, sometimes he's such a tool that I almost don't want to be his partner anymore. I shoot my grappling hook up to the top of the building next to me and prepare to go up.

"Kite." I hate the way he says my code name. In fact, I hate that code name. At least it's not so gravelly this time.

"It's 'Raptor' now. 'Red Raptor'."

"Right. I keep forgetting." *Yeah, sure you do. More like you're so mad I changed it without your permission that you refuse to accept it.* "Plus, until it gets approved by—"

"...by the Guild, it's not 'official'. Yeah, so you keep reminding me. Is there anything else?"

He tosses me a package wrapped in newspaper. The guy's a billionaire, and he can't splurge on some gift wrap?

"Happy birthday." Dude, something strange is going on for sure. And who gets the newspaper anymore?

"Uh, thanks." This is so weird I'm not even sure how to respond. I just look at him, waiting for something else. As usual, he just stands there being all tough and silent.

I thumb my grappler button and rise up toward the rooftops. As I turn around, I see Harrier pick something up off the ground and examine it in the moonlight...some kind of business card.

And I can't shake the feeling in my gut that whatever has him acting so weird has got to be really, really bad.

* * *

I change on the roof of my crappy apartment building as usual and take the stairs down to our apartment on the top floor. That feeling is still nagging me. What was it about Harrier that was so off tonight? That he was so nice to me for once? Or was it something else?

I haven't been home all day. I have an excuse ready to go, but then I realize it won't be necessary as soon as I walk in the door. Mom's asleep on the couch. No big deal at 11:00 at night, right? Maybe she was waiting up for me.

Yeah, right.

Except the only reason the bottle of vodka she has nestled against her chest hasn't spilled is because it's just about empty. And the only reason the cigarette in her other hand didn't burn our building down is that the ashes fell onto a plate sitting on the floor.

I start to think she's forgotten my birthday again, until I notice what's on the plate: a cupcake covered in wax from the melted candle planted in the center of it. Guess I should've stopped by after school before going out on patrol.

Underneath the plate is a homemade birthday card with a balloon drawn on a regular piece of paper folded in half. "To Sawyer"—by the way, my real name's Sawyer, did I mention that?—"Love, Mom." Hm. Don't usually get that much from her. That's almost as strange as Harrier giving me a present.

I grab the cigarette and the vodka and toss them, then take the thin blanket off the back of our ratty couch and cover Mom up. I decide to try a bite of the cupcake, so I pull the paper off the bottom and take a bite that isn't covered in wax.

Then I gag. Maybe the wax would be an improvement. Well, at least she tried this year.

As usual, it's up to me to clean up the mess in the kitchen even though I didn't cause any of it. The dirty dishes have been sitting here so long that they've become science experiments, and I just can't take the smell any more. Maybe I'll discover the next wonder drug if I test some of this stuff on the rats that live in our walls.

Then it's off to my sanctuary: my ten-by-ten bedroom with a twin bed mattress on the floor and a desk made from cinderblocks and plywood. I open the laptop—-the one I told Mom everyone at school got thanks to a new government program—-and type in my password: "redR@ptor15." That's a name I can live with. Being called "The Red Kite" made me feel like I'd never be taken seriously. I mean, nobody even knows it's a bird. I do need to change the number to sixteen before I forget, though.

As usual, the first thing I do is check for any news on Osprey. Like me, she patterned herself after The Black Harrier in her look and style. Unlike me, she isn't directly connected to Harrier. In fact, he's pretty irritated by the whole idea of a girl going out and copying what he does.

If he knew I was into her, he'd freak the eff out. Which is why I do my "homework" on her at home.

No new articles or blog posts, but on the main fan website somebody did manage to get a shot of her with his phone. It's not all that clear, but I can still make out the bottom half of her face under that white mask of hers. Man, she looks good in that costume. I think I'll save this pic for later. You know...for my research.

I leave a couple of comments on the message boards, fishing for some info on where I can find her. It's never worked before, but you never know when something might be helpful.

Yeah, I know it all sounds kind of stalker-ish, but what am I supposed to do? It's not like there's some clubhouse where teenage costumed heroes hang out so I can introduce myself to her.

As my computer shuts down, I remember the gift from Harrier and grab it from my backpack. Tearing off the paper, I can see right away that it's a new cape.

Black. What a surprise.

But as I unravel it, I realize something is different. The edges turn rigid when they're snapped out. And the new utility belt that's with it has...what are they? Jets?

Okay, I totally have to check this out. Now.

* * *

Back up on the roof in my new suit, I try to figure out how this tech works. It seems to be kind of like one of those base-jumping suits. It looks like the cape extends into a sort of glider and attaches to my gloves with magnets. And I think I can use the jets in short bursts to keep myself high up. Let's give it a shot.

I start out slow and jump off the AC unit on top of my building. As the edges go rigid, I'm able to float down. After a couple more tries, I start to get the hang of it. Harrier and I have used gliders before, but those were big, bulky rigs. It's a lot different when it's my actual cape.

Standing on the edge of the roof, I look out over the city. Millions of people going about their lives, most of them never giving a thought to the people like Black Harrier and me who are out there protecting them every night. From up here, it actually looks pretty nice, with all the lights. It's up close where you can see the filth and grime that it really starts to suck.

Most people would probably hesitate at this point, but I didn't become a masked crime fighter because I was afraid of trying things. So I drop my helmet visor, leap off of the rooftop and extend the cape. I'm able to stay in the air long enough to reach the building across the street, then I press the palm control for the jets to move higher just as I start to descend.

Nice. I could get used to this.

Let's see how high I can go. I head toward the nearest skyscraper and circle up to the top. It's an older building, probably built in the '30s, and has those convenient ledges that Harrier likes to perch on like he's one of those stone gargoyles. I stop on one to take a short break, then take a dive off the edge, a good fifty stories above the street. I blast the jets again and straighten out. At this height, I could probably glide across half the city.

I close my eyes and feel the air blowing against my face, and I realize I've never felt more free in my life. No mom, no school, no Black Harrier, no worries. Just flying through the night sky above the city lights. If I start getting around this way, I might miss the fun of getting across the city parkour style, but I think it'd be worth it.

As much as I'd like to do this all night, I realize I have school tomorrow and it's almost one a.m. Better head home.

I stay at a decent height to practice some more, figuring I'll circle down to my apartment building when I get close.

As I'm coming up on another skyscraper near my apartment, I realize I'm not going to clear the huge building so I tap the palm control again.

Nothing.

I'm out of fuel.

I try a sharp turn to get past the building, and it looks like I just might make it, but a gust of wind pushes me back just enough at the last second and I smack into the corner.

Ow! That effing hurt.

Now I'm in freefall. And it feels like I'm about to pass——-

Wham! Something collides with me, and for a split second I think I'm hitting the ground sooner than I expected. Or maybe the side of the building again. But instead of being, like, *dead*, I'm heading back up somehow.

Must be Harrier. He was spying on me. I can't believe that. I mean, yeah, he probably saved my life, but that is so not cool that he was still spying on me.

"Hold on. We're almost on the roof."

Wait. No gravelly voice. That wasn't Harrier. That wasn't even close to Harrier.

As soon I feel myself lying on a rooftop, I do what anyone would do after an experience like that. I throw up.

A lot.

At the absolute worst time possible, too. Because when I look up at my savior I immediately realize that I'm finally face to face with the woman I love.

Well, technically we've never met. But I still love her.

Osprey.

"What happened? How did you..." My voice is hoarse and sore from puking. I sound almost as ridiculous as Harrier.

"I spotted you flying around and wanted to check out how you were doing it. At first I lost sight of you, but then I saw you coming back around." So. Freaking. Beautiful.

"Well, I... Thanks. Thanks a lot."

She smiles at me and my stomach flops around like a fish. I can't believe she looks even better in person. Her costume is so much like Harrier's and mine, only...tighter. And white, with not as much body armor. "No problem. Just be more careful with your new toys next time. Mind if I...?" She gestures at the new gear.

"Go ahead."

Osprey looks at the edges of my new cape, then checks out the small jets on the belt. She leans in close and all I can think about is my breath. Is my breath okay? Omigod, I had that chili dog for dinner tonight. Better hold my breath.

I need a mint. Why don't I have any mints? I need to add a mint compartment to my utility belt.

"Pretty sweet, but not much room for fuel. Which I'm sure you realized a few minutes ago as you were plummeting toward the pavement." She laughs, and it's the most beautiful sound I've ever heard.

"Uh, yeah. Makes sense, really. It would be way too heavy otherwise."

"Harrier's a smart guy. He's got it all figured out."

Why do I feel so jealous? Of course she worships him. She's practically his stalker.

But obviously she's been keeping an eye on me also. I smile just thinking about it.

"Yeah. I guess he does." My throat's still hoarse. Probably will be until I drink some water. "So. You, uh, patrol around here much?"

"Just recently. I've been going around to different areas. Getting to know the city better."

"Oh. That's cool." *That's cool?* I'm a badass freaking crime fighter, why do I sound like such a dork? Get it together. You're going to blow this.

I try to think of what to say next. And nothing comes to mind. Absolutely nada. The awkward silence feels like it lasts for days. I realize I'm staring at her like an idiot, and I probably still have drool all over my chin.

Finally, she breaks the silence.

"Well, you take care of yourself. Next time I might not be spying on you when you get into trouble." She grins at me and shoots her grappler across the street. It looks like the same design Harrier and I use, attached to the bracers on our forearm.

"Wait!" Geez, could I sound any more desperate? "Do you think some time we could... I don't know... patrol together or something? Maybe tomorrow night?" Smooth, a-hole. Real smooth.

"Sure, why not? But what would The Black Harrier have to say about it?"

I make a way-too-exaggerated wave of dismissal, along with a lame sound like air leaking out of a tire. "It's not like he's my dad or anything."

"Okay, it's a date then. I'll meet you here at eight." She thumbs the button on her grappler and disappears into the night. Then I remember I have vomit all over my costume.

And my breath.

TWO

School.

Much worse than fighting crazy villains.

I purposely play dumb with my teachers so they don't expect too much out of me. I can live with Bs. And I don't need my guidance counselor trying to stick me in some AP class because she found out how smart I really am.

Same with athletics. Nobody knows how good I am at sports, especially gymnastics and wrestling. Otherwise I'd be spending all my free time after school practicing with a team.

There is one thing I'm not afraid to excel at in school, and that's technology. Between my computer class and robotics club, I get to play around with things I'm working on during school hours without drawing any attention to myself. I've been able to make some pretty cool modifications to my costume and utility belt. I even came up with the prototype for the retractable grapplers we use to get around the city, although Harrier was able to create much cooler ones based on my original idea.

But even there I don't really fit in, because the tech geeks see me as just some skater dude who listens to loud music. But the skaters think I'm a poser. And the popular kids don't even notice me.

I'm pretty much invisible to just about everyone here. And that's just the way I like it. Who needs a bunch of friends always calling up, seeing if I want to go hang out at... I don't know, like, the mall or whatever? Not me.

And, it's not like I'd have the time or the money to take any girls out on dates. That's why I don't bother asking anyone out.

Yeah, *that's* the reason.

For example, here comes the hottest girl in school—the captain of the cheerleading squad, Fabiola. All the girls trailing behind her in her entourage are almost as hot as she is, too. They're walking right by me when my skateboard falls out of my locker and rolls right in front of them. They step right over it and keep going without even looking in my direction.

See? That's me. I just show up in my plain t-shirt and jeans, no popular brands or band names plastered all over my clothes, nothing to draw attention to myself. I keep a low profile and blend in with the crowd. It almost always works.

Almost.

Unfortunately, there's always some Neanderthal whose hobby is to spot invisible people like me and make us his next victim. My personal caveman's name is Logan, and I'm pretty sure his parents actually named him after the guy with the claws from the comics. Except this guy only has the bad attitude without the Bushido code and dry wit to go with it.

He's also a lot taller than the Logan in the comic books. In fact, he's the tallest kid in school. He plays center on the basketball team and fullback on the football team. He's also the catcher on the baseball team, and I'm pretty sure he doesn't need to use a mitt. Obviously that doesn't leave a lot of time for stuff like homework, but it doesn't seem to bother anyone else. Not even the teachers or administrators.

As long as he can manage to juggle his various sports schedules, what difference does it make if he actually learns anything?

I showed up on his radar a few weeks ago when he was picking on a kid smaller than me, and I decided to get in the way. He was tormenting this poor guy, and everyone was either too indifferent or too scared to do anything about it. Even though I made it look like an accident when I got in the way, it still drew Logan's attention enough that he abandoned the other kid and made me his new "buddy." Obviously, I could pretty much destroy him in two seconds, but like I said, I try to stay invisible.

So I let him think he's pushing me around, and just make sure he never actually connects with a punch or shoves me too hard into a locker. I've watched enough action films to know how the stuntmen do it in fake fights, but it looks real to everyone else, including Logan.

Meanwhile, the smaller kid who I saved, Javier, has attached himself to me in kind of an annoying way. We definitely don't hang out after school or anything, but he tries to sit with me at lunch and stuff. And he isn't much of a conversationalist. I try not to be mean, but a lot of times I find myself trying to lose him or make an excuse to get away.

Today he sneaks up on me in the hall like a little ninja.

"Hey!"

"Hey, Javi."

"Um...did you...do your math homework?"

"Yeah."

"Me too! How about history?"

"I did all my homework. No need to go down the checklist."

"Yeah, I finally finished it all, too. I was up until almost 9:30 working on it. I thought my mom was gonna kill me for being up so late. Maybe we could——"

Suddenly Javier freezes like a rabbit who just spotted a wolf. His eyes widen as he stares past me and starts to get this weird twitch.

I turn around and spot Logan coming toward my locker, and mentally prepare myself for the idiocy. Javier scurries off in the opposite direction like the rodent he resembles. One of Logan's minions tries to trip him, but he manages to dodge the guy's leg and gets away.

Logan invades my personal space as he towers over me. I act as casual as possible under the circumstances.

"Guess what day it is today, loser?" Logan makes sure he's loud enough for everyone in the hallway to hear. And they do. Everyone in the vicinity is now staring in our direction.

I should just stay quiet and play dumb. But I don't. I'm simultaneously pissed off from dealing with Harrier and my mom and flying high from meeting Osprey, and it seems to be messing with my head.

"I'm pretty sure your mom said it was her birthday when I was with her last night."

This slightly infuriates Logan, especially when everyone else, including his friends, laughs so hard at my answer. They start egging him on, asking if he's going to take this crap from someone like me. He grabs the front of my shirt in his huge hand.

"Wrong. It's the day you finally get your ass beat." His face is red. Like, redder than my costume red. He shoves me into my locker.

"What's the matter? Did I wake you up when I was sneaking out of her bedroom?"

He swings. I move. He ends up punching a fist-sized impression into the locker.

Enraged and in pain, Logan screams. The crowd scatters as campus security rushes over. I might be able to get away, but there are too many witnesses around, so I'm going to get busted anyway.

So much for my "powers of invisibility."

* * *

"Logan, your parents are on their way to pick you up and take you to the emergency room. The school nurse thinks your hand may be broken." The principal, Mr. Blanchard, looks very sympathetic toward him, even though he knows Logan regularly bullies kids smaller than he is. I know he knows, and he knows that I know he knows. But he still doesn't do crap about it.

Logan just nods. I think he's trying really hard not to cry from the pain, and he's afraid his voice might crack.

"Sawyer, we can't seem to be able to get a hold of your mom." He pauses for me to respond. I don't. "We just have the one home phone. Is there another number where we may be able to contact her, such as a cell phone?"

Did you try Riley's Pub? "No, sir. I'm not sure where she is." I try not to look at Logan, who's holding his bandaged hand and staring me down like a pit bull on a leash. Whenever the principal isn't looking at him, it's like he's ready to rip my throat out with his teeth.

"A work number perhaps?" *If she had a work number, it would be on the freaking student information card that it took me an hour to fill out at the beginning of the year.*

"No, sir. She, uh...she's between jobs right now." I see the side of Logan's mouth go up in that combination sneer-grin he does so well, and it makes me want to beat his—-

"Then we'll just have to hold you in the office until after school. We can't have either of you walking around campus after such a display, since it would give the appearance that you did nothing wrong and that there were no repercussions." Mr. Blanchard used to be in the Marines before he became a P.E. teacher and, eventually, a principal. He still acts like he's in the military—and looks like it, too.

I look around his office at all the sports memorabilia, trophies, pennants...does this guy actually give a damn about education?

"What exactly *did* I do wrong? If you don't mind me asking."

Mr. Blanchard looks confused as to how I *could* ask such a question. "Logan's injury could cause him to miss a significant part of the season. Surely you understand how serious that is."

"Yeah, he punched a locker because I ducked. How is that my fault?"

"Several witnesses—-trustworthy students, I might add—(*in other words, Logan's popular friends)*—-heard you making inappropriate comments to purposely anger Logan. Obviously he was unable to control his emotions."

"So you're saying that my witty retorts to his threats were somehow just as serious as him trying to take my head off with that meat hook of his?"

Mr. Blanchard is saved from trying to justify himself by a knock at the door. His secretary walks in.

"Logan's parents are here to pick him up." She looks sympathetically at Logan's hand, then shoots me the stink eye.

"Tell them to come right in."

When I see the worried look on Logan's mom's face I almost feel bad. Then I remember the sociopath she raised and it goes away fast. She immediately starts to dote on him and help him out of his chair. He plays up the injury for his mom, and she totally buys into it.

His dad seems to kind of know better. He actually looks pretty angry at Logan. "I hope this doesn't affect your scholarship chances, son." Logan's mom gives his dad the *shut up or you're cut off for a long time* look.

He turns to the principal. "Thank you. We'll be back tomorrow for the meeting."

"See you then." Mr. Blanchard looks worried, too.

Again, I know I should keep my mouth shut. Again, I can't help myself. "It was nice seeing you again, Mrs. Andrews."

Logan's mom gives me a confused look, which totally makes sense since we've never seen one another before in our lives.

Logan turns back and his look tells me I'm a dead man once his hand is better.

But it was worth it. Totally worth it.

THREE

The Aerie.

That's literally what Harrier calls it. As if the whole bird of prey theme isn't stupid enough already, he actually has a name for a place that practically nobody else knows about except for me. And he couldn't keep it simple and call it "The Nest" either. It had to be a fancy name for it. I've never had the heart——or the guts——to tell him that actual black harriers have their nests on the ground.

Not that I mind being here. Harrier's penthouse is nice enough, sitting on top of the tallest building in the city. Douglas Tower has the best restaurant in town on the ground floor, along with a few high-end shops. The next several levels are offices, including Douglas Industries. And then the upper section is reserved for the most expensive condos in the city, with the top few floors belonging to Harrier.

But the secret level above the penthouse, that's a whole different thing. The fastest computers I've ever seen, a helipad that lifts when the ceiling opens, and more high-tech gadgets than an E3 convention. The entrance from the outside allows me to come and go without people wondering what a teenager is doing here all the time, and Harrier to enter and exit while in costume.

There's also a pretty amazing gym, where I'm currently working on the new moves Harrier showed me to improve my fighting skills. I almost hate to admit it, but everything he shows me does make me better. It's been that way all along. No matter how good I feel like I am, he's always able to help me improve.

The coolest things here are the various Black Harrier costumes, lined up in their plexiglass lockers. One for every occasion: fighting, detective work, base jumping, scuba diving, even climbing around in the sewers. Some are lightweight for stealth, others are heavily armored. But they're all mostly black, with some gray thrown in. And they all have the white on the underside of the cape like an actual black harrier, only to be seen when he's swooping down out of the air.

The only thing I don't like about this place is the shrine to the two previous Red Kites. I'm not even sure how he gets those costumes to stand up like that...almost like they're on invisible mannequins. They simultaneously make me feel like a poser and make me worry about what's in store for me.

"I thought I was clear about how I felt regarding that woman." Harrier never bothers to look up from his super-computer when we have these talks, as if I'm simply a distraction he's trying not to pay too much attention to. I mean, okay, so he's probably doing something super important, but he could at least act like we're having a conversation. And——so annoying——he's clacking away at a keyboard from, like, the '90s or something. He can *so* afford the latest in touch screen and even holographic technology, too. But, of course, he prefers the "old fashioned" way.

"She's not that much older than me. I wouldn't exactly call her a woman."

He actually stops typing for a second.

"What would you call her then?" He's got me there. Girl? Chick? Smoking-hot super-heroine?

"Why can't you give her a chance?"

He's back to typing again. "She's unsanctioned."

"By who?" Uh oh, here it comes.

"*Whom*. By me. By the law. And, most importantly, by the Guild."

"Yeah, yeah. Definitely don't want to be stopping crime and saving people without your union membership card, right?"

"Stay away from her."

"Okay! I got it." I hit the practice dummies extra hard, since I can't actually take it out on Harrier. I'm sure he notices.

"I need your help tonight."

"I'm busy. I have a project due at school tomorrow."

"The project can wait. This can't."

"It's going to have to. I'm already missing some assignments in science class, and if I don't turn this in, I'm going to be failing."

"And?"

"*And* I don't want to fail science."

"Then I'll handle it by myself." Sometimes I'd prefer it if he'd just yell at me. These stone-cold statements followed by icy silence are almost unbearable.

I barely get three more kicks in before I feel too guilty to stay quiet.

"Look, maybe I can help out for a couple of hours, then—"

"I'll be fine." Geez, I thought only women pulled this passive-aggressive crap. My mom's an expert at it.

"Are you sure? I—"

"In fact, maybe you should go now. Get a head start on finishing your...science project." Now's my chance. Take it. Take it. Take it.

"If you say so." I turn to leave the Aerie.

"Say hello to Osprey for me."

I freeze in my tracks and swallow hard. He knows. *Of course* he knows. I'm too ashamed to even apologize to him. I turn around and notice for the first time what he's working on: up on the screen is a photo and intel on his former arch-enemy, Pierrot. Stupid name for a super-villain, I know. Apparently he named himself after some sad clown from an opera or something.

But why would he be looking him up? Pierrot blew himself up before I even started working with Harrier, so I can't think of any reason he'd be working on this.

And then it hits me again: that nagging feeling that something is wrong, and this time it's like a panic attack. I clench my teeth and try to insist I'll go with him, but the words just won't come out. I stand there for about thirty seconds, trying to do the right thing.

Instead, I open the hatch and glide out into the evening sky without even looking back.

* * *

Things with Harrier weren't always like this. When I first became his partner, I was in awe of him. Before The Black Harrier existed, this city was like a war zone with all the criminals and gangs terrorizing everyone. He brought order and justice, and did it almost single-handedly.

I didn't know it at the time, but Harrier was really a billionaire named Franklin Douglas III. He went around town like a carefree celebrity, but he was hiding the fact that he had never gotten over his dad's death. His mom had died giving birth to him, and his dad raised him alone until he was killed by a gang of criminals when Frank was a teenager. When he was young, he was reckless, out of control, even after his dad died. But something made him turn his life around and dedicate himself to fighting crime.

I still don't know what that was.

I met him by accident. It was just after my thirteenth birthday, and I was skateboarding home from school. Some bangers in my neighborhood whose crew I had refused to join jumped me and pulled me into an alley. They were going to give me a serious beating. Maybe even kill me.

They surrounded me and smashed my board in half. Then their circle started moving in, and they were shoving me between them. No matter how much danger I've been in since then, it's never approached the fear I felt at that moment. I was sure I was dead.

Suddenly, Harrier appeared out of nowhere, which was strange because he's very rarely out in the daylight. He told me to run, and I almost did. But then something happened. As I watched him fight, I suddenly felt like I could do the same thing. After about a minute, I had seen enough of his moves that I decided to try some.

The next thing I knew, I was bending a guy's leg backward with a kick to the knee, then breaking the jaw of another guy with a palm to the face. There I was, fighting back-to-back with my hero. It was amazing. Exhilarating. I'd never felt anything quite like it.

I had found it really easy to learn tricks on my board if I saw someone else do it, or watched a video. But it still felt like I was learning it on my own. Maybe it was the surge of adrenaline, or the feeling that I had become powerful enough to take on those guys, but this was something on a whole different level.

Harrier noticed, and I thought for sure he was going to yell at me to run again. Instead, he stood there and watched me take out the last two guys by myself.

I couldn't see his eyes behind those tinted lenses he has in his mask, but it was obvious that he was doing some serious thinking. He walked over and stared at me for a long time, like he was assessing my worthiness or something. Then he questioned me about myself and my life. I had no idea at all what was going on, but I wasn't about to lie to him or keep quiet. He'd just saved my life.

Finally, he asked me if I'd like him to train me to defend myself. It didn't even take a second for me to respond. Was he kidding? Of course I wanted the best fighter in the world to train me to fight.

The rest is history.

* * *

Of course, the one time I really need Mom to be gone or passed out, and she's wide awake watching some stupid reality show. Instead of putting on my costume and sneaking up to the roof, I have to change up there and stash my clothes somewhere.

I sling my backpack over my shoulder and try to cross the room as quickly as possible.

She turns down the volume on the whiny voice of some so-called reality star. "Where are you off to?"

"Library. Science project."

"I need to talk to you about—"

"Sorry. Gotta go." I close the door before she can get out another syllable and rush up the stairs to the roof before she can follow me.

Before I put on the costume, I sniff it to make sure it doesn't still smell like puke. The bleachy smell from that cleaner I used isn't much better, but it'll have to do.

I always wonder when I'm changing like this if someone in one of the nearby buildings ever spots me and wonders what I'm doing. Not that people in the big city care much about what other people do, but it would definitely be weird if they did.

As I'm putting on my new cape I think about Harrier again. What's he doing tonight that he would need my help? He's never asked me like that before. In fact, I've been having to go out on my own more than ever lately.

After making sure my costume's in order, I glide across the street to the building where Osprey and I met. The butterflies in my stomach and weakness in my limbs actually make me second-guess the idea of patrolling with her. What if I'm not focused enough? I could actually get killed out there.

But as soon as I see her waiting for me I know there's no way I could cancel on her. The way she looks, the way she stands, the way her costume...

Anyway, she doesn't seem upset that I'm a little late thanks to Mom, so that's good.

"Kite."

"Hey, Osprey." Did I sound okay? Stay cool. Stay. *Cool.* "I actually go by Raptor now. Red Raptor."

"What was wrong with Red Kite? I kind of liked it."

"Nothing, as long as someone knows it's a pretty awesome hawk. But most people think of a toy that flies in the air."

Osprey laughs. "I have to admit, I did think that when I was a kid. But I guess that was a different Kite back then. When did you take over?"

"I'm actually the third. I've only been his si—partner for a few years."

"I never realized that. What happened to the other two?"

"I wish I knew. He won't talk about it." And I've asked. I've asked a *lot*.

"That doesn't sound good."

"Yeah. Tell me about it. That's the other reason I wanted to change my name. I don't like having to live up to what those other guys did." It feels good to tell somebody this. I certainly can't tell Harrier. But why am I trusting her so much? I really have no idea who she is or what her real agenda might be.

"How'd you come up with the new name?"

"I don't know. It just kind of came to me." *Liar.* I spent hours trying to find something that wasn't either already taken by a real crime fighter, or trademarked by some comic company or movie studio.

"Red Raptor. I like that too. But now you have a similar problem to the one you had with Kite."

"What's that?"

"Everyone might think you were named after a dinosaur instead of a bird of prey."

"Yeah, I guess. But it's a lot better than a diamond-shaped toy on a string."

"So... where should we start?" Every time she smiles at me like that, my chest tightens. What is up with that? I clear my throat to make sure it doesn't crack.

"Ummm..." *Grab some dinner? See a movie? Followed by some serious making out?* "Whatever. Where do you usually go?"

"Well, I have my earpiece tuned in to the police scanner. When I hear something's going on, I try to beat the cops there."

Wow. Awesome. How come I never thought of that? "Yeah. That sounds pretty good." I do my best shrug. I wish I could see her eyes, but she has those same reflective lenses in her mask that Harrier uses.

"Hold on a sec." She puts a finger to her ear and listens for a moment. "Okay, got something. Corner of First and Adams."

Before I can respond, she leaps off the roof. Sure enough, she's already copied the design of my new cape and she's gliding toward First Street faster than I can keep up. I don't see any jets, though. That'll probably only take, like, another week or so for her to tackle, from what I know about her.

I leap off the rooftop after her, and realize I still need to practice this some more. I'm used to jumping around on rooftops and swinging from my grappler line. Gliding through the air is a whole different thing, and since I haven't seen someone else really do it, I have nothing to imitate. It's definitely fun, though.

I'm moving too fast to see the looks on the faces of the people below, but I can see them looking up and pointing at us. Some of them are recording us on their phones. I bet we make the papers tomorrow.

Too bad nobody reads the papers any more. Maybe we'll be all over social media.

As I follow her, I start to fantasize about her being my partner instead of Harrier. We could be together all day and hang out, then patrol at night. Then we could go home and— whoa! I need to pay attention. I almost hit that power line and fried myself. Definitely need to focus.

But what would happen to Harrier? Would he just go on alone? Find a fourth Red Kite? Why do I really care? Most of the time, he just acts like I'm a pain in the ass anyway.

We arrive on the scene, but I have no idea what to expect. All I see is a building with its alarm going off and broken glass everywhere. When Harrier and I work together, we always have a plan. Osprey apparently just jumps in and improvises.

As we get closer, I can see that it looks like a typical jewelry store robbery. Bust through the window, get in, grab what they can, get out fast.

Unless Harrier and I happen to get lucky, we don't usually come across this kind of action. Osprey lands outside the entrance to the store just as the first masked robber exits with his bag full of goodies. She smashes him in the face with a roundhouse kick before he even notices she's there.

Another advantage of the new glider cape is that I'm moving pretty fast when I slam into the next guy out the door, and he's out cold with no more fuss. Osprey gives me a big smile, which unfortunately means I'm not paying attention when a third guy takes a shot at me with his pistol.

Luckily, his aim sucks and the bullet whizzes through my cape without touching me. I hope I can fix it well enough that Harrier doesn't notice, or I'll wish the bullet had gone through my heart.

I toss one of the throwing stars from my belt at his gun, and it lodges in the end of the barrel, just like it's supposed to. As I leap forward and knock him down with a foot to the face, I recognize the mask he and his buddies are wearing.

No. This is *not* good. They're the henchmen of—-

"La Cucaracha!" Osprey calls him out like we're in a cartoon or something. It's the first thing she's ever done that I didn't totally love.

My instinct is to run. To call Harrier for help. But I don't want to look weak in front of Osprey.

"I don't believe we've had the pleasure, *mija.*" I'm not sure the guy under the costume is even Latino, but he always throws in some Spanish words to keep up his shtick. Why someone so huge would name himself after an insect never made any sense to me, but I'm pretty sure super-intelligence isn't one of his powers. He's all strength, and looks like one of those Photoshopped bodybuilder guys who are too huge to be real.

"It's Osprey. And meeting me is going to be one of the *least* pleasurable experiences you've ever had." Witty banter. I like that. Usually Harrier just grunts and barks orders.

She leaps straight at him, and he just smiles under that *luchador* mask he wears. As pumped up as he is on steroids and whatever that experimental adrenaline serum is, she doesn't stand much of a chance against him on her own.

It's a good thing I'm here with her.

She swings her collapsible staff at him, and he grabs it away from her with no effort whatsoever. Then he bites down on the middle of her staff, pulls down on the ends, and snaps it into three pieces with his mouth.

As La Cucaracha swats Osprey away, I throw one of my smoke bombs at him. Best if he doesn't know where I'm coming from.

While he stomps around in confusion, I help Osprey up, and she looks pretty flustered. She's also holding her arm like it's injured. I don't think she has any experience fighting actual super-villains, and she's probably embarrassed by how easily he took her down. I get the impression that, up until now, this has been some kind of game to her.

"Come out, *parajito*, and face me." His chest and arm muscles bulge out so much as he pumps his serum that it rips his costume.

I keep my voice low even though he probably wouldn't hear me over his own bellowing. "Get ready to slam into him from the back. I'm going to come in low and sweep his legs."

Osprey nods at my plan and moves around behind La Cucaracha before the smoke starts to clear. I run straight at him, then turn sideways and roll the last few feet into his shins. Osprey hits him in the back just at the right time, and he falls forward like a bowling pin.

His face slams into one of the display cases and it smashes to pieces under his weight. We jump out of the way as glass shatters all over the place.

Any normal person would be lucky to be alive after that. I'm pretty sure we just pissed him off. He struggles to get up and screams with rage.

"He's too strong. We need to disconnect the serum. I'm going to distract him. You try to grab onto those tubes and yank them out." I make sure Osprey nods her understanding, and then rush the big bug again.

I try to land a kick to his face, but he grabs my leg while I'm in the air. I know people talk about someone's grip being like a vice all the time, but his really is. There's no way I can break it. He swings me around in a move like he's in a wrestling ring, and tosses me through the front window of the store. Despite my disorientation, I manage to wrap myself in my cape before I skid across the sidewalk and into the street.

One of the first things Harrier taught me was how to land without getting hurt, so I'm in pretty good shape as I try to figure out my next move. I just hope Osprey—-

No. He must have caught her as she tried to pull out the tubes that deliver the serum. La Cucaracha holds her up with one hand around her neck, Darth Vader-style. With that grip, she doesn't have long.

Since his back is to me, I should have one chance to do this. I run and flip through the gap in the storefront window, landing just behind him. With two throwing stars, I cut the tubes going into the back of his neck from the canisters on his belt.

He immediately screams and drops Osprey. His veins turn blue, and his skin flushes as his muscles start to atrophy and shrink.

45

I hear the sirens as the cops finally show up. I'm really not in the mood to give a report right now, and some police officers really don't appreciate us doing their jobs for them. I help Osprey up again, then tie La Cucaracha up just in case.

Then we take off out the back door.

* * *

Patrolling with Osprey for the first time takes me back to when I first started with Harrier. I had no idea what I was doing, and he had me stay off to the side and observe for a long time before he allowed me to get in on the action. I was still in my regular clothes then, so nobody suspected I was with him.

Meanwhile, he was training me at The Aerie and showing me all the moves he knew. Since I picked up everything so fast, it was just a matter of going through all the different styles of fighting and then practicing them for a week or so. His style is a combination of a bunch of different martial arts and fighting techniques, but he wanted me to learn everything from the easy beginner moves up to the most complex combinations for each discipline.

Within a few months, I had so many choices every time I made a move that it was kind of overwhelming. But soon I narrowed down the hundreds of options to certain ones that I liked and were the most effective for me. My style isn't even the same as Harrier's. I use a lot more kicks, but he prefers punching most of the time. I think it's part of his anger management program.

It wasn't all just training me to fight, though. Harrier also became my mentor. I never had a dad around growing up, and even though he isn't much of a father figure, he's still a strong role model for me. He's helped me to learn other things about life that I just haven't gotten growing up with a single mom.

Plus, he bought me practically anything I wanted or needed. The only problem was that most of the time I couldn't bring it home.

Eventually, he gave me my Red Kite costume and made it official. It was pretty close to the others' costumes, but there were some modifications and improvements, and I've made some changes of my own over the past three years—-adding stuff to the utility belt, even changing the symbol. One thing that's always consistent is the red, black, and white coloring.

There's a popular joke among crime fighters that the heroes like to dress their sidekicks in bright colors so they make better targets and keep the heat off of them. But I don't think that's true, at least in Harrier's case. I think the red is so that I always stand out no matter how many people are around, so he can keep an eye on me and make sure I'm safe.

At least, that's what I always tell myself.

* * *

"Thanks for saving my butt back there." Osprey seems pretty sore as we cross another rooftop. I can't glide with the bullet hole in my cape, and she probably isn't in any shape to be doing it either.

"No problem. I've fought the guy so many times with Harrier I didn't think it would be that big of a deal. I guess sometimes I don't realize how much I still have to learn."

"What's it like? Being his——"

"Sidekick?" I *hate* that word.

"I was going to say 'partner'."

"Oh. Sorry. Little sensitive about that, I guess."

"Why?"

Do you have a few days to talk about it? "It isn't easy living in the shadow of someone like The Black Harrier."

"I'd give anything to be his partner."

Not sure what to say to that. But I remember feeling the same way once. "Yeah. It's kind of one of those, 'Be careful what you wish for' type of things, you know? When I first started working with him, I was in awe. But just like everything else, it wears off."

"I guess I really don't know what it's like for you, but I can't imagine ever getting sick of it. He must teach you so much."

Now I'm feeling guilty. What is my real problem with Harrier? Is he really that bad, or is it me? Am I being an ungrateful little brat?

"Um, yeah. I guess he does."

We arrive back at our meeting place, too battered to do any more patrolling. Osprey walks up close to me and reaches out, then wipes some blood off of my face.

"Thanks for showing me a good time, hero."

Omigod omigod omigod, is this really going to happen? Is it? She leans in close, and I close my eyes. Then she kisses me.

On the cheek.

I open my eyes, and she's already backed away. Osprey holds out her hand.

"Hey, before you go, I have something for you." That smile. God, I love that smile.

"Really?"

She tosses me a small tin box. I look at the front: Not just mints—-the really strong mints. I'm not sure whether to be insulted or hopeful.

"You might want to keep them in your utility belt." She shoots her grappler at a nearby rooftop and zips away into the night.

* * *

I'm so up from my night with Osprey that I don't even notice that the light from my bedroom is shining under the door before I open it.

Mom's there, sitting on my bed. Arms crossed, cigarette in hand, blowing smoke out her nose like a dragon. At least there's no bottle this time.

"Where the hell have you been?"

"I was out."

"Out where?" She stabs the cigarette out and drops the butt into an empty diet soda can.

"Just out. With a girl." *Since when do you care?*

She rolls her eyes. "I hope you used protection. The last thing you need is to be paying child support for the next eighteen years."

"Mom, it's not like that." *But I sure wish it was.*

She stands up and gets in my face. "You think I'm stupid?"

"Well, you did manage to get knocked up when you weren't much older than me, didn't you?" Oh, man, that was dumb.

She slaps me across the face. Not in a child abuse sort of way. More like an old-timey-black-and-white movie sort of way.

Still hurts, though.

"I shouldn't have said——"

"And where'd you get this?" She pulls out my older, spare costume and shoves it at me. I couldn't be more shocked, and I'm sure it shows on my face. My heart pounds like it's holding a sledgehammer and it's trying to break out of my chest cavity with it.

"That... that..."

"Must have cost a fortune. Just for some stupid costume party, or...or comic book convention." The relief is so overwhelming that I almost collapse into a puddle of goo.

"But——"

"I called the school today about your computer. They said there is no government program, and they don't know where you got it from. And this." She tosses something at me and I almost don't catch it in time. "This...i-thing——"

"Tablet." Damn, I thought I had that hidden pretty well.

"Whatever it is, it's even more expensive than the laptop.

I think it's pretty obvious what's going on here."

"It is?" *Wait.* So did she figure it out or not?

"You're selling drugs."

I can't help it. I bust out laughing. I really need to learn some self-control.

"What's so funny?"

"You think I'm... I'm..." I laugh some more. What I don't think about is how disrespectful this must sound to her.

"You stay out until all hours. You come home with bruises and cuts that you can't explain. And you buy all these expensive things when we don't have any money. What else can it be?"

Hmmmm. Good question. What else could it be?

She lights another cigarette. "Things are going to change. I'm getting my act together and so are you." This causes her to think twice about her new cigarette. She looks at it, then smashes it out.

"What?" I can't believe where this is going. How did things turn so crappy so fast?

"Plus, we're meeting with your principal tomorrow. Something about you hurting some football player?"

It just keeps getting better and better.

* * *

The meeting does not go well. Mr. Blanchard makes it sound like I should have stood in the way of Logan's fist in order to cushion the blow. My mom actually agrees. After all, she was a popular cheerleader in high school before she got pregnant at only eighteen during her senior year.

She even apologizes to Logan's parents.

For the next month, I get to spend my lunches each day cleaning up trash to learn my lesson. Across the conference table, Logan manages to smirk at me only when nobody else is looking at him. He must practice that a lot.

After Logan and his parents leave, the meeting changes focus to my "underachievement." Apparently my aptitude scores were off the charts, so the only way I could be doing this badly in school is laziness. Me. Lazy. Right.

When the new semester starts next week, I'm going to be placed in honors and AP classes, and I'll be expected to work extra hard to catch up. I'll also be placed in a special program for "at risk" kids, where I get free tutoring after school and for a few hours every Saturday. And, to top it off, my mom is going to start dragging me to church on Sundays, followed by Bible study.

I'm totally screwed.

FOUR

P.E. class.

Hate it. I ditch it the next day figuring I can't get into any more trouble than I already am. Not only is Coach Carmichael my least favorite teacher, but it's right before lunch. This is the only chance I'll have to tell Harrier I won't be around for a while, since my mom found my phone and took it away, assuming it was part of my dark, shadowy secret life slinging drugs. I can't call Harrier from a landline, because I have no idea what his number is. It was pre-programmed into the cell phone he gave me, and there was some kind of app on there that masked the number.

So I head to The Aerie as quickly as I can, hoping I can be back before lunch ends after P.E. so I don't have to miss English class also.

But when I get there, he isn't around. I check everywhere, and even go down to the penthouse in case he's still asleep after a long night patrolling. No luck. And his bed doesn't look like it's been slept in.

I guess he could be at some kind of board meeting or something at Douglas Industries, but it's rare that he shows up for those kinds of things. He always lets Mr. Chen——the one other person he trusts besides me——take care of all the business stuff.

Then again, maybe he just got lucky. I did see him on TV a couple of days ago, out on a date with that one actress. I can't think of her name, but you'd know her if you saw her. She's been in a bunch of stuff.

He pretends the billionaire player thing is just an act, but I know him well enough to see that it's the one thing he actually enjoys about being a handsome rich guy. Frank Douglas is usually at the top of any "most eligible bachelor" list, leaving even the most popular movie stars and athletes in the dust. As a matter of fact, he beats out Black Harrier, since nobody knows they're the same person.

I teased him about it once, but after the harsh over-reaction I got from him, I never brought it up again. The way he acted, you would've thought I made a joke about his dad being murdered or something.

Back in The Aerie, I look around the place and feel like I should have enjoyed it more when I had the chance. This place has everything, and I just took it for granted. Why do people always do that? I promise myself that if this blows over and things go back to "normal"——I can't help but smile at that word——then I'm going to appreciate being here a lot more.

I leave Harrier a message on the desktop of his giant computer screen to make sure he doesn't miss it. I tell him I'm not sure when I'll be able to go back to crime fighting, or when I'll even be able to contact him.

I leave out the fact that I'm starting to feel like I may never see him again.

* * *

The next couple of weeks are the worst ever. It's all about going to school, improving my grades, and being punished for stuff I never even did. Plus, Logan's always mad-dogging me and making sure I know he's my stalker now, even though he's waiting to actually get his revenge. His hand wasn't even broken, and it's getting better fast. Now he just has to wait for the right time.

And it turns out I did get into even more trouble for ditching P.E. Now I'm the towel boy for the wrestling team on top of everything else. And three guesses who the star of the wrestling team is.

Actually, I bet you can get it in one.

At home, Mom has been staying sober and going to AA meetings. I never thought I'd be mad that she got her act together——actually, I never thought she'd get her act together at all——but it's the worst time ever for me. Suddenly she thinks she's super-mom just because she makes me some toast in the morning before school and isn't passed out drunk when I get home.

She also doesn't currently have any boyfriends, something which has definitely been a constant joy in my life. Most of the guys are complete losers who make her look like a great catch, and the ones that aren't are obviously only after one thing——and that thing isn't something a kid wants to think about when it comes to his mom. More than half the time they're married or have serious girlfriends, which has led to endless fights between my mom and other women, and even some of them showing up to our apartment at all hours demanding to know where their men are.

To make matters worse, we live in a one-bedroom, so when she does have a guy over, they're either in the middle of the living room or——grossest of all——in my bed.

A few of them have even tried to hit me, but once I learned to fight, that came to an end. They never tried it in front of my mom, so that left me free to break some wrists, noses, and ribs before these ass-hats knew what hit them.

To top it all off, she's making a little extra money now by watching the neighbors' little kid while they're at work, which is a lot. In fact, I think they pretend they're at work quite a bit more than they actually are to get a longer break from him. So in addition to not having any privacy, I have the little monster running around the house when I get home. And the shows he watches...with those songs that get stuck in your head...I literally feel like I'm going insane.

Meanwhile, I don't see Harrier, I don't see Osprey, and I don't get to do any crime fighting. In fact, without my tablet, my phone, and my laptop I feel like I'm living in the Stone Age.

And between my mom's reality shows and trailer-trash talk shows and the little ass-wipe's cartoons and annoying sing-song crap, I can't even watch the news.

I'm totally out of touch.

* * *

One day after wrestling practice is over I'm getting ready to put away the mats when I hear someone approach from behind me. From the heaviness of the footsteps, I correctly assume it's Logan.

Everyone else has hit the locker room already, and the coach is in his office. Logan's had the bandage off his hand for a couple of days now, so I know what's coming. The difference is, this time he can't have any witnesses because of what happened last time.

"Hey, loser." I can hear the sneer in his voice.

I try to ignore him, knowing that it isn't going to work.

"Hey, I'm freakin' talking to you. Turn around."

I turn around slowly and face him. As much as you can face someone who's more than a foot taller than you, anyway.

He looks down at me, his lip curled into a snarl. He even looks like he's shaking like a crazy person.

"My hand is better. It's time to do this." He makes a fist and punches his own palm to illustrate his point.

"You don't want to do this, Logan."

"What the eff are you talking about?" He looks at me suspiciously.

"I don't want to hurt you again."

He laughs. "You didn't hurt me, loser. I hurt myself. But this time there's no locker, and I'm not gonna miss."

He swings and I easily step out of the way. But as he loses his balance, he decides to barrel into me with his shoulder, a move so stupid that I wasn't prepared for it at all.

We both fall to the mat, and he tries to get on top of me. He's actually a really good wrestler, but I'm...well, you know. I turn him around and grab his arm, twisting it behind his back. Then I tap a pressure point that paralyzes him.

"Had enough?"

I guess he hasn't. "You better freakin' kill me, 'cause I *will* get you for this."

How do you even deal with a psycho like this? Obviously I can't kill him. What am I supposed to do?

"Gentlemen!" Coach Carmichael really knows how to yell. "What's going on here?"

I look up, and he's standing in front of the entire wrestling team, most of whom have a look of disbelief on their faces.

"Uh... Logan was just teaching me some wrestling moves, Coach." I let go of his arm and jump up. Logan collapses onto the mat.

"Well, he must be quite a teacher. I've never seen anyone pin someone who outweighed them by so much like that."

"I, uh... I'll just finish with the mats and the towels, sir."

"Forget the towels! You're an official member of the team now." The other wrestlers look at one another in shock.

When is this hell going to end?

FIVE

Snacks.

Everyone needs them, especially after the slop they serve at lunch in the cafeteria. While skating home from school I stop at the mini-mart on the corner for some junk food. Luckily, mom still hasn't found the debit card Harrier gave me for things like this. I grab a bag of my favorite spicy chips and an energy drink and head for the checkout, but I notice something's wrong.

The guy behind the counter has his hands in the air, and there are five guys a little older than me grabbing the money out of the register and anything else they can carry. I look up at the security mirror and see that three of them have guns pointed at the guy.

They haven't noticed me yet, so I decide to take them out as quickly and quietly as possible. I crouch down and silently approach them from behind. But the clerk blows it by looking directly at me as I'm about to attack, and the bad guys immediately turn around and point their weapons at me.

Now it'll probably get messy.

I jump on my board and throw my energy drink at the furthest one from me, and it explodes all over his face as it hits him in the nose. In a split second, I'm right on top of them. Now that I'm closer, I grab the gun arm of the guy closest to me and spin him around so that he's in front of me. Luckily, I'm right in thinking that his friend isn't going to shoot him to get to me. But he does try to shoot over his friend's shoulder and hit me in the face with the bullet—-except he fires wide and it smashes the glass on the refrigerated display nearby, busting a forty-ouncer, which sprays all over the place.

This upsets the clerk so much that he actually starts yelling at the shooter, which is about as stupid as stupid gets. The only good thing about it is that the guy turns to point his gun at him instead of me, which will give me a chance to get him.

I hit a pressure point on the guy I'm holding and his knees turn to jello, then with a swoop of my legs I have the shooter down on the ground. A quick hit to the face and he's out cold, leaving only two more to handle.

Leftover punk number one goes to shoot me, so I kick my skateboard up into my hands and swing it at him. It knocks the gun out of his hand, which allows me to take him down with a combo move. Four down, one to go.

Number five is too scared to shoot. He drops his weapon and just looks at me, which is a reaction I get a lot from someone who's seen me take down several of his friends. I start to smile, but then I realize I don't have my mask on.

And then I recognize this kid from my history class. We stare each other down for a few seconds. Then, as if an unspoken agreement has taken place, he nods at me and runs out of the store. That's when I notice there's someone else in the store with us.

I turn and look down one of the aisles, and Javier is standing there with his mouth hanging open and his eyes popping out of his head. Crap. He must have been following me around again. How am I going to get rid of this kid?

He looks like he's afraid of me for some reason, and he takes off running out of the store.

Before I can go after him, the clerk starts berating me in a language I don't understand, as if stopping a robbery and possibly saving his life isn't enough.

He's mad that I messed up his store and let one get away.

* * *

So now not only am I stuck on the wrestling team, but some kids from my school know I'm not what I appear to be. I wonder if any of them have the brains to put together that one of their classmates is able to take down criminals the same way as the famous teenage sidekick who operates in the same neighborhood. I doubt those goons are very bright, but Javier could be a problem.

So what happens to me if everyone finds out I'm Red Ki—-er, Raptor, anyway? Do they lock me up for assaulting so many people, even though they all deserved it? Do they give me a medal for helping to put so many criminals behind bars? Do the police throw me into an interrogation room and question me until I give up the identity of The Black Harrier?

I have no idea.

While other kids my age are worried about having a sweet pair of kicks, or getting rid of that zit on the end of their nose before their date Saturday night, these are the things I have to think about. Hiding my secret identity. Pretending to be a loser who sucks at everything in life. Oh yeah, and trying not to get murdered by some super-villain.

I walk in our front door and mom is making dinner. It appears to be an attempt at spaghetti, only the sauce looks like ketchup and there are cut up hot dogs in it instead of meatballs. I know I shouldn't be so picky, but Harrier usually gets us takeout from the best restaurants in town. It's not only healthy, but delicious. I'm going to have a hard time keeping this stuff down.

The brat she babysits doesn't seem to have a problem with it, though. He's scarfing it down like he hasn't eaten in days, and it's all over his face. When he opens his mouth to show me what's in there, I gag.

"Have a seat. I'll get you some." Mom's actually proud of this crap.

I sit down on one of our rickety, mismatched wooden chairs, and the rugrat stares at me from across the tiny table, still chewing with his mouth open. All of a sudden, he stops eating and closes his eyes. The next thing I know, he sneezes right at me, spraying me with snot and bits of food.

Totally disgusting.

My mom, of course, doesn't even notice it's all over me. "Bless you! Sawyer, you might not want to get too close to him, he's pretty sick."

I do my best to wipe everything off me. "Yeah. Thanks for the warning."

Mom dumps some of her pasta-ish stuff into a plastic bowl and sets it down in front of me. For the first time in my life, I wish we had a dog just so I could feed it under the table.

Except that might be cruelty to animals.

"How was school today? Practice go okay?"

I decide to tell her since she's going to find out soon enough anyway. "Coach, um, made me part of the team."

"What?" She really could have turned down the shock a little bit to spare my feelings.

"The wrestling team. I'm on it now." As much as I hate the situation, I have to admit I enjoy telling her now that I see how low her expectations are for me.

"That's...amazing. How did it happen?"

Can't tell her the truth, that's for sure. "I just tried a couple of holds with some of the guys after practice, and the coach said I was pretty good."

"Huh. Well, I certainly wasn't expecting that to happen. But good for you. I'm glad you finally found something you're good at."

Ouch. Not that I'd know from personal experience, but moms aren't supposed to talk to their kids this way, are they?

I take a drink of the watered-down grape Kool-Aid she gave me to wash down the bad taste in my mouth. From the food and her comments. It doesn't help.

"That's not true. I'm good at...at..." *What?* Go ahead and tell her: Krav Maga, Kung-fu, Karate, Tae Kwon Do, Judo, Jiu-Jitsu, Muay Thai, kickboxing, nunchackus, acrobatics, computers, detective work, parkour, swinging from rooftops...

She raises her eyebrows, waiting for an answer. The kid is staring at me, too, snot running down his face.

"I don't know. *Stuff.*" I stand up and set my bowl in the sink, then stomp off to my room like a three-year-old. Why am I so upset? I've spent years covering up the fact that I'm so good at everything. Is it really unreasonable that nobody thinks I'm good at anything at all?

As I'm passing the TV, which mom must have left on after her show ended, I spot Harrier in the little box above the news anchor's right shoulder. I stop and turn up the volume to see what she's saying, since the brat is singing some song from one of his shows at the top of his lungs back in the kitchen.

The story is about how Harrier hasn't been spotted in a couple of weeks, and the crime spree that seems to be resulting from it. Harrier has done this before when he had missions in other countries or went deep undercover, but I decide I should probably look into it anyway. If the local news has noticed and is concerned, then maybe I should be too.

I decide to try and sneak out tonight to check on him, but it'll have to be late. Since my mom doesn't have a regular job, she sleeps a lot during the day and stays up most of the night to make sure I'm in bed. But at some point, she has to get tired and nod off, right?

SIDEKICK

* * *

I jolt awake with a start, and realize I was the one who got tired and nodded off. And, right away, I figure out why. Headache, chills, clogged sinuses, sore throat. That little germ incubator got me sick.

I look at my clock, which is blurry from the sleep in my eyes, and see that it's after 3:00 a.m. After listening at my door for any sign of mom being awake, I open the door and head for the bathroom.

Uh, yeah...heroes have to pee, too.

It takes a lot of effort not to sneeze, but I can't wake up mom. I check on her from the hallway, and she's snoring away on the couch with the TV playing an infomercial about some food processor.

Back in my room, I put on my costume and sneak out the window. It's not something I like to do, because if someone spots me they'll know exactly where Red Raptor lives——at least if they see me changing on the roof, they only know which building it is——but I can't risk waking up mom trying to sneak out the door.

I climb up the fire escape and stand on the edge of the roof. The cold early morning air is fresh and makes me feel a little better, and I take a deep breath before plunging off into the darkness. My cape snaps out and I glide down the street at about fifty feet up.

It feels so good to get out in costume that I can't help stopping for a mugging I see along the way. Some lady going in to work early is having her purse taken away by a couple of guys with shaved heads and more metal in their faces than a scrapyard. Not much of a challenge, but I'm a little out of shape. Should be fun.

I swoop down and stomp the guy holding her purse with both feet, sending him into a twenty-foot slide ending in a stairwell. As soon as I land, I grab the purse from the unconscious mugger and turn back to the victim, assuming the other guy will be running away as fast as he can.

Unfortunately, I'm wrong.

He has the lady in a headlock, and holds a knife up to her face. Suddenly this isn't so fun anymore.

I start to reach for one of the throwing stars in my belt, but he's watching me carefully, with the paranoid eye of someone on some serious drugs. He touches the blade to the woman's face. "Move and I cut her."

I lift up my hands. "Okay, man. Stay calm."

"Give me the purse." His hand shakes, which makes me nervous that he's going to cut her whether he means to or not. "Slide it over here. Now!"

I toss the purse over to him and it lands next to his feet. I can tell he wants to pick it up, but he's afraid I'll attack the second he no longer has the knife up to his victim.

He's right, but I try not to let him know that. "Just pick it up and let her go."

"How do I know you won't follow me?"

"You have my word. Just don't hurt her, and you can leave."

"Your word don't mean crap to me." He thinks for a second. And it turns out this guy is smart. "Take off your mask."

"What?" It's so unexpected, it doesn't even register at first. How did this go downhill so fast?

"Your mask. I wanna see your face."

"I can't really..."

"Now." He pushes the point of the knife against her face, and it draws a little blood.

I have no idea how to handle this. Heroes and villains have an unwritten code where we don't do this type of thing. If everyone finds out our identities, the whole thing is over. But this is just some low-level street thug.

"Okay, okay. Just stay calm." I lift my visor and pull my mask off, and he just looks at me. "Happy?"

He looks disappointed somehow. He shrugs.

"What were you expecting?"

"I don't know. You're just some kid." I'm not sure why I'm insulted. That should be exactly what I wanted to hear. He probably won't even remember what I look—-oh, no.

The mugger pulls his phone out of his pocket with his other hand and holds it up to take a picture of me. "Say cheese."

His phone flashes and he hits a few keys.

"Here's the deal. I just got a text ready to send your pic to my woman. If I see any sign that you're coming after me, all I have to do is hit 'send'."

He slowly reaches down with his knife hand and picks up the purse. "You be a good boy, and all I do is hold on to it for insurance."

He throws his victim to the ground and starts to back away, his thumb hovering above the 'send' key. Once he's halfway down the block, he starts to laugh and shouts to me. "Then again, I might be able to get a few grand from selling this to—"

THWACK! A boomerang flies out of the alley and knocks the phone out of his hand, followed immediately by a bolo that binds his ankles together. He falls flat on his face, and I see a tooth bounce out of his mouth as his jaw hits the sidewalk.

I quickly replace my mask and run over to the victim to see if she's okay. She starts thanking me profusely, but I don't hear a word she's saying as I watch Osprey walk out of the alley and step on the mugger's neck. In my mind, it's like she's moving in slow motion.

"I hope you have better insurance than that, because you're going to need it." She kicks him in the face and he's unconscious. After picking up some things that fell out of the purse, she walks over to return it. I don't hear anything the lady says to thank Osprey either, and I realize I must look pretty ridiculous standing there with my mouth hanging open. I just hope I'm not drooling.

I shake my head and walk over to grab the guy's phone off the ground. Looking at the screen, I can see that the text hasn't been sent, and I breathe a big sigh of relief.

After deleting the picture, I pull off the back and yank out the memory card, then stick it in my utility belt so I can destroy it later. I pull out the battery and toss it into the sewer drain. The rest of the phone I throw to the ground hard and stomp on it until it's completely destroyed.

The lady tells us she's fine and that her work is only about a block away, so we watch to make sure she makes it okay.

I turn to Osprey, and I'm so happy to see her, but at the same time embarrassed about everything. "So...I guess you saved me again."

"That's right. So we're no longer even. I guess I'll have to think of a way for you to pay me back."

"I'm sure you'll think of something."

"You know...I've been coming by this neighborhood a couple of times a night for the past few weeks hoping to see you."

"Yeah. About that..." What am I supposed to say? *My mommy grounded me from crime fighting?* "I've been working on an important assignment, and it's been keeping me really busy."

"Are you sure? Because I was afraid that maybe you didn't like me or something."

You could not be more wrong about that. "Oh, no, no, no. That's definitely not it. Not it at all."

"Is this special assignment the same reason Harrier's been missing also?"

Well, I certainly can't tell her I have no idea where my mentor's been all month. "Uh, yeah. Kind of. In fact, I'm on my way to see him now."

She perks up when I say this. "How about I come along? Then we can call it even again."

"I really wish I could. I'll talk to him and see if he'd be okay with you meeting him some time." Sure. *Like when hell freezes over.*

"Promise?"

"Of course. Thanks again for your help." I go in for a hug, then immediately feel weird about it and we do the awkward dance. I decide to shake her hand instead and she gives me a weird look. So I shoot my grappler across the street and get out of there as fast as possible.

Ugh. I'm such a freaking loser.

* * *

I think about what I'm going to do if I don't find Harrier. I don't have a lot of time to go looking for him right now. I could try to contact the Guild, but I'm actually not too sure how to do that. It's not like I have a number for them. Or an email address.

The Guild was started several years ago by masked crime fighters who felt that some threats were too big to handle individually. But most of the time, they're just more adults making rules for no reason. If someone wants to fight crime, they should be able to fight crime without getting permission from anyone.

I've only met most of the members once, at a meeting Harrier brought me to in order to introduce me to them. He put a blindfold on me so I wouldn't know where their headquarters was located—something about not being able to reveal the location if I ever got captured and tortured or brainwashed. To be honest, the fact that they even consider that a possibility makes me kind of nervous. Anyway, I was excited about going and meeting these people.

But even then, some of the members weren't there. Cupid, the archer guy who flies, was pretty cool. And the super-speed guy, Fastlane, was really funny. Bast caught me looking at her chest, and just smiled and winked at me. But most of them acted like they couldn't care less about meeting me. Firefly and Omar the Defenestrator were even hostile toward me.

In a way, it's like getting a bunch of movie stars together in a room. They act like they get along, but you can feel the tension because they all have such big egos and they're trying to figure out who's more important. I guess it's hard for them when they're so used to being the most popular person in the room. They all claim to be doing what they do because they want to help people, but I don't think anyone could do this without some level of self-importance and overconfidence.

Maybe even mental illness.

Some of them have their own sidekicks, and I know Harrier doesn't care about *them*. So I'm not sure how they'd react to me contacting them even if I could figure out how to do it.

Just another example of Harrier treating me like a kid. Because he doesn't give me access to information, I'm wandering around in the dark now that he's not around. How am I supposed to grow up if he never trusts me or gives me any responsibility?

* * *

Entering The Aerie, it feels cold and abandoned—lights are off, heat's off, totally silent. Scratch that...I do hear something coming from the control room. I assume it's Harrier, but just to be on the safe side I move in quietly.

There's someone standing at the main computer, and it's definitely not Harrier. With everything dark except for the computer screens, the figure is just a silhouette, and I can't tell much other than that he seems to be in a costume. I can tell that he's somewhat smaller than Harrier, but still bigger than me.

I climb up onto the metal support beams above so I can literally get the drop on him. As I wait to make sure he hasn't noticed me, I can't see much more than I could before. Whoever it is had no problem getting into Harrier's system, so he must be really good at tech stuff. I go through a list of enemies who might have that capability, but none of them match the dark figure I see below. Either way, it's sort of a good sign, because most of the geeky villains who can handle that sort of thing aren't so good in the combat department.

I hop down and prepare to knock out the intruder, but I don't even come close. Before I can touch him, he casually grabs a staff that he has leaning against the terminal next to him and knocks me into a wall.

Whoever this guy is, he's good. I toss some throwing stars at him as a distraction since I know he's going to knock them down, then do a flying kick at his head. He slaps me and the stars out of the air with almost no effort, then kicks me back up against the same wall, knocking the wind out of me.

I can only hope he's not out to kill me, because it looks like he'll be able to without missing a beat.

He approaches me, and now that my eyes have adjusted I realize who he is: Redhawk, a hero I've never met who lives in another city. Why would a hero break into Harrier's base?

"You ready to talk, or do you want to keep sparring?" It sounds like he finds the situation humorous.

"Redhawk?"

"And you're the new Kite, I presume?"

"It's Red Raptor now. And I'm not sure three years qualifies as new."

"Has it really been that long?" He smiles. "Red Raptor. Not bad. Are you worried people are going to think you're supposed to be in Jurassic Park?"

"Maybe a little. But it's better than 'Kite'."

"Oh, you don't have to tell *me* that." He holds out his hand. "I'm Alex, the original Red Kite."

* * *

Redhawk explains everything to me, including how he became Harrier's first sidekick. It started shortly after Harrier began his crime fighting career, when he realized he was going to need help.

Alex was a teenager who was part of the police explorer's program and wanted to become a police officer. He was also a black belt in more than one form of martial arts, as well as a boxer. He had been interested in fighting crime ever since his parents were killed in a restaurant during an organized crime hit. He was actually sitting at the table with them at the time, but didn't get hit.

During a charity benefit for the orphanage where Alex lived, Frank——Harrier——started talking to him in his civilian identity. Alex had been performing some stunts as part of the benefit, especially using his Bo staff, and Harrier was impressed. Harrier began sponsoring Alex in competitions, and training him in other forms that he knew.

Harrier eventually let Alex in on his secret, and allowed him to tag along on patrols. At first, Alex just wore a ski mask and body armor, but after a while, Harrier had the first Red Kite costume made for him. I had always assumed the first Kite had come up with the name himself, but according to Alex, Harrier picked it out for him. Alex had wanted to call himself The Red Hawk from the beginning, but Harrier thought it sounded too Native American or something.

* * *

After the history lesson, Redhawk confirms what I already suspected: He believes Harrier's disappearance has something to do with his investigation of Pierrot. He also fills me in on some important information I never knew about the relationship between our mentor and his most dangerous enemy. Pierrot was the one villain Harrier could never completely defeat. Could never capture. It started to drive Harrier to the edge of what he would normally do as a hero. A couple of times, Alex thought he might even break his hard and fast "no killing" rule when it came to the evil clown.

They never discovered Pierrot's true identity or his motivations. He wasn't after money...in fact, most of his plans cost way more than he ever made from them. His purpose in life seemed to be to destroy Harrier—-not kill him, but destroy everything he stood for, and everything he did.

Most importantly, I learn that the second Red Kite died in the same explosion that killed Pierrot. That explains why Harrier never talks about him.

I ask Redhawk what Pierrot was like in person. He thinks for a second before answering. "You know the evil clown from *It?*"

"Yeah." I've seen him on TV anyway. Never read the book.

"Imagine that clown running away screaming from something that terrifies him. That something would be Pierrot."

I'm not sure I've ever shuddered before, but I do it now. "That bad, huh?"

"More evil than you can imagine. And the few pictures of him that were taken before he died don't do him justice. In those, he looks like a sad, fat clown. In person, he was scary as hell to look at. Especially his eyes."

"Is that why he dressed up like a clown? To fool people?"

"Are you kidding? A lot of people are terrified of clowns. Seriously...do a search for 'evil clown' sometime. He knew exactly what he was doing."

"Yeah, I guess it is pretty creepy." I remember going to a birthday party when I was little, and there was a clown there. Half the kids wouldn't stop crying the whole time.

"I'm going to hit the streets today and see if I can dig anything up. It's been a while since I did any patrolling around here, though. You think you might be able to go with me?"

"I, uh, can go later on tonight, but I kind of have school today, and I can't miss it."

"Then I'll do what I can on my own and you can join me later on."

Before I leave, I ask Redhawk if he'll train me with a staff, and he says it would take months or even years to get good enough that I'd be able to actually use it against criminals. I tell him about my particular talent, and he sounds intrigued.

Once we're in the gym, he shows me some basic moves and, even with my cold slowing me down, I pick them up immediately. Impressed, he gets more complicated quickly and I'm still able to keep up. Within an hour, he's shown me everything he knows, and I can duplicate it all perfectly.

I always wondered why Harrier never trained me with a staff, and I realize it's because it would remind him of Alex.

As we're about to leave, Alex suddenly has an idea and we head back to the control center to try one more thing. He opens a compartment on the main computer panel that I've never noticed before and types in a code, then presses a red button.

"Ever met Eaglestar before?"

I'm puzzled by the question of whether I've ever met the most powerful being on earth. It seems so random. "No. He wasn't there the one time I was at a Guild meeting. Why?"

"Because you're about to." He looks at my slack-jawed expression and grins. "Don't get too excited, though."

"Why?"

"'Cause he's kind of a douche-bag."

Just then, there's a sonic boom, and The Aerie rattles as if there was an earthquake. Redhawk opens the Helipad doors, and I see the most amazing thing ever. Eaglestar floats down from the sky, and hovers a couple of feet off the ground. His eyes glow, which creeps me out more than I would have thought.

Eaglestar was a World War II fighter pilot who shot down a lot of enemy planes and became a big hero along with his squadron. They were sent on a secret mission to take down an airship the Nazis were using to transport some kind of artifact——supposedly something of alien origin——and the rest of his squadron was killed during the fight. He managed to take down the rest of the planes escorting the airship singlehandedly, but ran out of ammo in the process. So he did the only thing he could, and rammed his plane into the ship, which erupted in a fiery explosion.

But instead of being killed in the crash, he was given extraordinary powers, including super strength, invulnerability, flight, apparent immortality, and the ability to shoot some sort of energy out of his eyes. At first the government used him as a secret weapon to help win the war——and hunt down the Nazis who also gained powers in that explosion——but it wasn't long before the word got out. Now he's the world's greatest hero, and everyone loves him.

Then again, everyone hasn't met him in person.

"Where is he?" With his strange, hollow voice, it's hard to tell if he's angry or not, but it sure seems that way.

I look at Redhawk nervously, but he doesn't seem fazed by this. "He's not here. That's why I called you."

"*You* called me? That signal is for Harrier. And only Harrier." Redhawk was right. He does sound pretty douchey.

"Yeah, well, Harrier has been missing for a few weeks. I was hoping maybe you could—"

"Harrier goes missing frequently. Cases in other nations, undercover work, that monastery in Tibet... there are also missions with the Guild, even off-world on occasion." Eaglestar sounds more dismissive than anyone I've ever heard.

"Is there currently a Guild mission in progress?" I can't believe Redhawk is talking to the guy this way. He scares the crap out of me.

"No."

"Then why bring it up?" Now he's even challenging him. Redhawk's got guts, I'll give him that.

"My point is that Harrier often disappears without warning, and he always returns. Why are you so concerned?" I wish he wouldn't keep floating that way. It's like he's too good to stand on the ground like the rest of us.

"Well, for one thing, his partner has no idea where he is."

Eaglestar turns his gaze on me as if he's noticing I'm there for the first time. I'm pretty sure I pee a little in my costume. "Has he ever performed missions or left the country without informing you of his whereabouts?"

"Well——" I have to clear my throat because my voice is cracking from nervousness. "He's done it once or twice... for a few days. And there were a couple of times he took... um... women on trips. Like, vacation?"

"Is that a question or a statement?"

Confused and flustered, I look to Redhawk for some help. He speaks up. "We don't think any of those situations is currently the case. We're not even sure he's alive. As I was saying, I was hoping you——"

"Until you have some evidence of foul play, I suggest you stop worrying. Harrier can take care of himself." Eaglestar starts floating toward the helipad doors. "And don't use that signal again unless there's a major threat to this city or a planetary emergency. I'm not at your beck and call."

"Sorry to bother you then."

He stops floating away for a moment and fixes his glowy, icy stare on Redhawk. "In the time we've had this conversation, three-hundred seventy-two incidents occurred in which I could have prevented a crime or an accident. Nine lives have been lost. If you believe you were simply 'bothering me' then you are mistaken."

Eaglestar takes off so fast that he's nothing but a blur, and a sonic boom follows. Redhawk closes the helipad doors.

"Well, then. I guess we're on our own."

* * *

I think about meeting Eaglestar the entire way home. I never thought that meeting one of my heroes could freak me out so much. Meeting Harrier was definitely a rush the first time, and even though that feeling eventually went away and he even started to annoy me sometimes, he's never treated me as badly as Eaglestar just did. I guess maybe I should give him more credit for the way he acts, considering who he is.

With Eaglestar I felt like I didn't matter. Totally insignificant.

Even though Harrier never introduced me to him, I knew they went on missions together and stuff, especially with the Guild. I kind of always assumed they were friends. But for him to not care at all that Harrier is missing and could even be dead...wow.

I manage to sneak in my window, strip off the suit, and climb under the covers just in time for mom to come in to wake me up for school. I try the old "too sick to go to school" routine, but even though it's for real, she won't have any part of it. It's a good thing I got several hours of sleep before I left, because this flu or whatever is starting to knock me on my butt.

As I ride my skateboard to school, my head continues to throb and my throat starts to feel like it's on fire. Great. So I'm supposed to go out searching for Harrier with my predecessor, and I'm going to look like an amateur because I feel like I've been run over by a truck. Redhawk's going to wonder why Harrier ever chose me as his new partner.

It definitely doesn't get any better once I get to school, either. All the loud noise in the halls makes my head hurt even worse, and it seems like everything is closing in on me.

After first period, Javier runs to catch up to me in the hall as I'm opening up my locker. I wonder if he's going to bring up the incident in the convenience store yesterday.

"Hey, are you okay? You don't look so good." He's acting normal. Maybe he isn't going to bring it up.

"I'm coming down with something. That kid my mom babysits sneezed and coughed all over me."

"So..." He seems kind of nervous now. "Yesterday at that store..."

Think fast. Why didn't I come up with a cover story? "Yeah, that was crazy, right? I had just finished an energy drink, and I've been taking these karate classes, and it's like I just went nuts with adrenaline or something." *You're sounding like an idiot. Shut up.*

"Yeah, it was pretty cool.

As I feel my nose tingle, I do the Dracula thing and sneeze into my sleeve.

So of course I have snot on my sleeve when Fabiola, that really hot cheerleader, decides to talk to me for the first time ever. "Hi. So I hear you're on the wrestling team now."

Even though the words she's saying are obviously about me, I still find myself looking around to make sure she isn't talking to someone else. "Um. Yeah. I guess I am."

"Does that mean you're coming to my party next week?"

"Party?" Of course I've heard about The Party, but I have to play it cool. Everyone is going to be there. Suddenly my invisibility doesn't seem to matter much anymore.

"It's a masquerade party. I'm going to wear the skimpiest costume I can find. Trust me: you don't want to miss it."

"I don't? I mean, yeah, I don't."

"Follow me online so you can IM me for directions. 'Kay?"

"Okay. Yeah. Sounds good."

As she's walking away, Fabiola grabs my arm for a second, and raises an eyebrow when she feels my bicep. Her mouth curves into a half smile and she doesn't break eye contact until she's around the corner. I keep watching the spot where she disappeared as if I can still see her through the wall.

Javi picks his jaw up off the floor as he stares after her also. "That-that-that was——"

"I know."

"And she, like, talked to you. And touched you. And invited you *to her house*."

"I know." I turn and close my locker so I'm not late for class.

He finally looks at me instead of the empty space where Fabiola went around the corner. "Are you going?"

Let's see: Black Harrier is missing, Redhawk wants me to help search for him, and even if I don't end up dead, my mom has semi-permanently grounded me and won't let me out of her sight.

"Probably not." As I walk away, I can almost hear Javi's jaw hit the floor again.

* * *

Algebra 2 is a difficult enough class for me to stay awake in even under the best of circumstances. But when I'm sick, stayed up most of the night, and had the prettiest girl in school talk to me, my concentration is as far from good as it can get. My head feels like it's a blown-up balloon, my throat is swelled up, and I have chills.

Mr. Cross's voice sounds like it's coming from a TV in another room as he drones on about variables or whatever. I keep going back and forth in my head between thinking about Harrier and trying to figure out a way to go to Fabiola's party next week.

I start picturing Fabiola in Osprey's costume. Then I actually start to feel guilty. But why? It's not like we're dating or anything.

I have to stop letting my mind wander like this. I need to pay attention in class or I'm going to be in more trouble. Then I'll never be able to help figure out what happened to Harrier. That gets me thinking about Pierrot. I've never seen a picture of him close up, but I start imagining him with glowing red eyes like Eaglestar's, and a tongue like a snake.

I go from feeling like I can't keep my eyes open any more, to suddenly realizing I'm being woken up by the teacher and the entire class is laughing at me. Worse, there's a puddle of mucus on my desk where I laid my head down, and a string of it stretching between the desktop and my face when I sit up.

When my teacher sees this, he quickly changes his attitude from annoyed to concerned. "Sawyer, maybe you should go see the school nurse."

"I think I'll be all right, sir."

"It's not a request. You look really sick, and I don't want to spend my weekend in bed or, worse, have my wife accuse me of getting my kids sick again. You need to go now."

I grab my backpack and head out the door, some of the other students still chuckling as I go. I'm so out of it I can hardly think straight, but I do start to worry about whether I'm going to be able to help Redhawk out tonight at all. Then I hear a loud clanking sound coming from around the corner, like metal hitting on metal. I can't figure out what could possibly be making that noise.

As I turn down the hall toward the office, I see Logan out of class, running down the hall and slapping all the combination locks hanging from the lockers as he goes. I secretly smile when I see Mr. Blanchard come out of the teacher's lounge, thinking Logan is finally going to get busted for something. But he completely ignores the racket Logan's making and heads straight over to me.

He gets right up in my face like he's about to kick my ass or something. His breath smells like old coffee and there are long hairs coming out of his nostrils and eyebrows in all directions. "Mr. Vincent, do you have a pass to be out of class?"

You've got to be kidding me. I point after Logan, and the loud clanking noise still coming from his direction. "Seriously? But——"

"Do you have a pass or not?"

I try to think through all the snot clogging my head as I feel around in my pockets. I come up empty, and realize I left the classroom in kind of a hurry. "Uh... I guess Mr. Cross forgot to give me one."

"We'll see about that." He starts writing out a referral slip. "Where are you going?"

"To see the nurse." I start to feel the tingling again, as well as an overwhelming pressure building in my sinuses.

"Are you really? You seem fine to me. Are you sure you're not——"

That's when it happens. The biggest, grossest sneeze I've ever had, and I can't get my hands out of my pockets in time to cover anything.

It explodes from my nasal cavity, all over Mr. Blanchard. Green slime is everywhere.

I try to hold back a smile as I apologize. "I'm really sorry—— "

He pulls out a handkerchief and starts wiping himself off, beginning with his face. "Just go! Get out of here. Now!"

I know it's mean, especially for a supposed hero like me, but I feel so much better after doing that. When I get to the nurse's office, it turns out she isn't even here today. Due to budget cuts, she's only at our school twice a week, and today isn't one of those days.

The secretary in the office tells me I look horrible, and to go lie down on the cot in the back of the nurse's office until she can get a hold of my mom to come pick me up. Knowing full well that she's never going to get ahold of her, I drift off for a nice, well-deserved nap.

* * *

Of course, once I'm asleep again, the dreams start up thanks to the cold meds I took this morning. Only this time it's not some weird metaphor thing, but a dream about the past.

In fact, it's so much like a "life flashing before my eyes" dream that I should probably be worried that I'm sicker than I thought, and I'm actually dying.

It's like watching an edited recording of my adventures with The Black Harrier, only instead of from my own point of view, I see everything from a distance. The early months of my training, going up against ordinary thugs on the street. Then my first encounters with costumed villains like Music Master and Creeping Death. Then the more dangerous bad guys such as Med-Evil show up, and things get really hairy.

As it goes on, I can remember how I felt all along the way. How the whole thing went from being a constant thrill to just hard work, and finally a job that I dreaded showing up to every night. But it wasn't Harrier who changed. It was me.

He was the same hero, with his drive to clean up the city and bring justice to criminals. He treated me the same way from the beginning to now. But I somehow lost that feeling I had when we started and started to act...what? Ungrateful? Like I took it all for granted? Like my life would be better if I went back to being just some lonely skater dude who tuned out life listening to heavy metal with my earbuds in and spent all my time after school practicing tricks on my board?

The school secretary wakes me up to tell me school's over and it's time to go home. It takes me a minute to shake out the cobwebs and get over the disorientation of having slept in a place I'm not used to. The cold meds and the sickness don't help, and the dream felt like it lasted for years.

An overwhelming feeling of loss hits me when I think about Harrier being missing. Just when I realize I should be happier with my situation as his partner, he might be gone forever—-and it could all be over with.

<u>SIX</u>

Crap.

That's the best way to describe what I feel like as I head for The Aerie. I had the unbelievable luck of Mom taking the brat to the theater to see some stupid 3-D kid movie, and because she could see how sick I really was, she left me in bed and trusted me to stay put.

Of course, when she gets home she'll probably figure out right away that the lump under my covers is just a bunch of clothes and not really me, but I'll have to worry about that later. This is way too important.

As if being half dead with the flu isn't enough, it starts pouring down rain as I head out to meet Redhawk. By the time I get there, I'm completely drenched.

I get to The Aerie even earlier than Redhawk was expecting. I enter through the hatch and he stares at me and the puddle that's quickly forming around my feet. I let out a big sneeze.

"You're not looking so good." Redhawk isn't just making an observation like everybody else. He seems genuinely concerned.

"Yeah, so everyone keeps telling me."

"Maybe you shouldn't go with me then."

"I'll be okay. I took a really long nap this afternoon."

He doesn't look too sure, but I have a feeling he really needs the help so he doesn't want to push the issue too much. As he grabs his equipment and starts to put his mask on, I happen to look over at the glass case with his and the second Kite's costumes. Now I know what happened to the other one, but Alex still hasn't told me why he left.

I decide this could be the only chance I have to ask him, considering how dangerous our mission is. "Hey, Alex."

"Yeah?"

"You don't have to tell me if you don't want to, but...I've always wondered why you stopped being the Red Kite."

Redhawk sighs and looks over at his old costume himself. He considers for a long moment, then points to one of the chairs in the control room. We both walk over and each take a seat.

"I don't know what your situation is, but I get the impression you have a real life outside of...this." He gestures around The Aerie. "That wasn't really the case with me."

"What do you mean?"

"I was an orphan when Frank met me, and all I wanted to do was train to become a cop and bring criminals to justice. He took me under his wing and trained me until I was more effective than I'd ever be as a police officer."

So far he hasn't told me anything I didn't already know.

"But what became even more important to me was for him to adopt me, since he was the closest thing I had to a parent in many years. He always made excuses about how a single guy couldn't adopt a teenage boy that way, but I know that he just never really wanted the responsibility. Someone as rich as he is can hire lawyers to make pretty much anything happen, you know?"

I never really thought about any of this since I already had my mom. That must have been hard on him.

"So I lived at the orphanage until I turned eighteen. Then I had to find someplace else to go. I kind of assumed I'd be able to move in here once that happened, but when I brought it up...well, you know how he can be."

"Definitely. But what was his excuse for not letting you move in?"

"He was worried about 'the appearance of impropriety.' I'm not sure whether he was more afraid of it scaring off the ladies, or the implication that would result from a young guy moving in with a rich bachelor like that."

It takes me a second to register what he means, just because it isn't something I would have ever considered. "Seriously? But it's not like you're——" I cut myself off when I realize I don't actually know if what I was about to say is true. But it's none of my business, and shouldn't matter anyway. What Harrier did was messed up. "I mean, it's not like you would interfere with his dating life or anything, right?"

Alex just smiles. He knows I'm uncomfortable, and for some reason he has no desire to alleviate it by telling me anything one way or the other. Which is fine. Because, you know——like I said——none of my business.

"So when I packed up my stuff and left the orphanage, I just kept on going and left town. Never even said goodbye to him."

Wow. So, that's nothing like I was expecting to hear. I don't know what I was expecting to hear, I just know it wasn't that. "Well, thanks for sharing. I've always been curious."

"Anyway, we have a lot to do, and that's all ancient history now. So, what do you say we go beat up some bad guys?"

"Sounds good."

When I try to exit from The Aerie the usual way, Redhawk just crosses his arms and shakes his head. "I have a better idea."

He takes me down a private elevator to a secret garage in a sub-basement under the building's regular parking levels. I feel pretty angry and maybe a little jealous that Harrier's never shown me this area, but there's no reason to get into it now. For one thing, it's not Redhawk's fault Harrier never told me about it, plus Harrier's not around for me to discuss it with him.

As the doors to the elevator open, the first thing I see is a giant black vehicle that looks like a cross between a Ferrari and a tank. How did I not know about this? Does Harrier not use it any more, or does he just not use it when I'm around?

But what Redhawk really wants to show me is parked behind the big vehicle: a set of motorcycles, a big black one and a smaller red one.

I guess my expression at seeing these gives away the fact that I had no idea they existed.

"What's the matter?"

"I just...I never..."

I can tell from his expression that Redhawk didn't realize I had no idea about this stuff. "He was probably just waiting for you to get your license. But you're old enough now, right?"

He shows me how to start the bike, and then throws me a dusty red helmet that was sitting on a nearby shelf. At first I have trouble just moving along on the thing, but then, like everything else, I get the hang of it from watching Redhawk. He's an expert rider, and it doesn't take long for me to replicate his ability.

Once I know what I'm doing, it's the most amazing thing I've ever done. Even better than gliding around above the city. I thought skating on my board was cool, but this is about a billion times cooler.

The helmets have mics and speakers in them so we can communicate. As we're riding, Redhawk tells me about the time after the second Red Kite was killed by Pierrot. He and Harrier hadn't spoken much since their falling out, but he went to visit him after the funeral. Harrier had stopped putting on the suit, and was spending all of his time sitting around his penthouse drinking.

He wasn't sure what brought Harrier out of his depression a couple of months later, but he did see news stories about Harrier and Red Kite together all of a sudden, so he always figured getting a new sidekick had something to do with it.

In other words, I somehow managed to drag him out of his despair. Not something I would have ever considered.

Out on patrol with Redhawk, it reminds me of the early days with Harrier. The main difference is that Redhawk actually has a sense of humor, even while fighting. I tend to throw in some comments here and there, but he goes at it all the way. At first I don't get why he would waste his time joking around so much with bad guys who obviously don't appreciate it. Then I realize it's a tactic. Not only do they not take him as seriously as they should, but I can tell they're really distracted and frustrated when he does it.

We race around town rounding up thugs and questioning everyone we can find who might know something. Word must get around fast, because soon whenever we catch sight of any criminal-types, they scurry away immediately like rats.

We do manage to catch a few, including one guy who's way too overconfident for his own good. As we approach and the rest of his gang runs away, he stands right in front of our bikes and flips us off with both hands and smiles. I toss him into an alley, my favorite place to take care of scum like him.

"I see you got a new boyfriend, Kite. Harrier getting too old for your taste?"

I hit him in the stomach. "What have you heard about Harrier?"

He has trouble talking with the wind knocked out of him. Guess I hit him a little too hard. "Nothing."

I hit him again, this time in the face. Then I grab him by the shirt collar and shove him hard against a brick wall. "I find it hard to believe someone in your line of work hasn't heard anything at all about this city's hero disappearing."

He wipes away the blood streaming from his nose and sneers at me. "I don't care if you believe me or not."

"My new friend here is just as anxious to find out some information. I'm going to let him ask a few questions now."

"Oh, I get it. The old 'good cop/bad cop' routine. It ain't gonna work, kid."

"I wouldn't be so sure about that. See, the thing is, *I'm* the 'good cop'."

He looks nervous as Redhawk cracks his knuckles and approaches him. Yeah, it's cheesy, but it's effective. I actually turn around because I'm feeling kind of nauseous, so I'm not really sure which bones Redhawk is breaking when I hear the cracking sounds.

* * *

After hours of not being able to get any good info, we finally have the name of a certain low-life snitch who supposedly knows something. Warren "Weasel" Wilson is never very hard to find once you're looking for him. Every cop in town knows to go to Weasel if you can't get anything out of anyone else, and every criminal knows to stay away from him because he's under the cops' protection. And Harrier's as well.

We confront Weasel as he's pulling a con on some tourists downtown. A bunch of people who don't know how dangerous it is to be in this neighborhood at night——or even in the daytime for that matter——stand around while he plays the cup game with the rubber ball on top of a cardboard box. A couple of the guys watching, who I'm sure he planted, win a few dollars, and the rest get confident and start throwing down fives, tens, even twenties.

I have to admit, he's pretty good. And from past experience, I know he's even better at lying than he is at getting people to hand over their money willingly. But with the right, ummm...motivation, I guess? He's definitely a pretty reliable informant.

Before we can even get close, Weasel has taken a couple hundred dollars from them. Since I'm familiar with the game, I pull the ball out from his sleeve, and the crowd starts to get angry. We make him give back the money as best he can, and most of the suckers are happy. Some of them probably even got back more than they bet.

After the tourists are done taking pics of us with their phones, we grab Weasel and take him into a nearby alley. For some reason, he's much less talkative than usual, so we decide to take him to a nearby rooftop to loosen him up some.

Harrier found out years ago that Weasel is afraid of heights, so usually as soon as he's uncooperative we grab him and pull him up top, and he starts to sing. But even after I take him on a little ride with my grappler and we're on the edge of a high building, he's still tight-lipped. That's when Redhawk decides to pull one of Harrier's favorite moves and hang him upside-down from the ledge.

From the smell, I can tell immediately that Weasel has crapped his pants, but he's still afraid to talk. Redhawk and I both lean over him as he hangs there, looking straight down at the pavement ten stories below. Redhawk tries to get him to open up a little more, this time playing the "good cop" part.

"What are you so afraid of? You know you're untouchable in this town. Harrier's always had your back."

"Harrier ain't been seen in weeks. Who's gonna help me when—when—when... *someone* comes after me? The cops are afraid to leave their patrol cars lately."

"Well, maybe if you help us out, we can find him and he can protect you."

"I-I-I-I don't think that's gonna happen."

"Why?"

"I can't tell you, man. Please."

That was my cue to be "bad cop." "Let's just drop him, 'Hawk. If he won't talk anymore and he isn't any help finding Harrier, then what good is he?"

Redhawk looks like he's having too much fun with this. "I don't know, Raptor. It's a long way down."

"I know. I want to see what happens. Besides, once everyone he's ever snitched on realizes nobody's protecting him anymore, he's going to be dead anyway."

Even with our bad acting, Weasel is terrified. "Wait! Maybe you guys can ensure my safety, huh? Like, keep me somewhere safe until things blow over."

Redhawk grins at me. "That sounds fair. Now tell us what you know about Harrier's disappearance."

Weasel starts shaking, and at first I think it's just because he's so scared of us dropping him. Then I realize he's sobbing uncontrollably, and it's because of what he's about to tell us. "Pierrot has him."

Redhawk couldn't have looked more shocked if he found out Santa Claus was holding Harrier at the North Pole. But instead of expressing shock, it comes out as pure anger. "Pierrot's dead."

"Yeah, well...I guess he got better."

My turn again. "You better not be lying to us, or next time we hang you from the top of Douglas Towers."

"I swear, man. I swear. I seen him myself."

My mouth is so dry, I have trouble getting my next question out. "Is Harrier alive?"

"Last I heard. But word is, he won't be for long."

"Where is he holding him?"

"I don't know. Somewhere nearby I think. But you better bring backup."

"Why?"

"'Cause Pierrot's gathered all the big time crooks in town to work for him, and some from other places, too. In fact——"

BLAM! A bullet goes right into Weasel's forehead and through the other side. I almost throw up right when it happens, but I don't need Redhawk and Osprey both thinking I can't stomach being a hero, so I manage to hold it down.

Almost too far away to see, I catch a glimpse of the assassin repelling down the side of a building, sniper gun still in hand. It's hard to tell at this distance, but I'm pretty sure it's Deadeye. If it is, I'm not sure why Redhawk and I are still alive. He's such as good shot, and so fast, he could have taken down at least one of us before we even knew what was happening.

I guess we really couldn't protect Weasel. Whoops.

We glide down to the street as fast as we can, since the next shot could still be for Redhawk or me. We jump on our bikes and speed off in the direction of the shooter. Deadeye is on a bike also, so we're pretty far behind him thanks to his big head start.

I try to remember everything I know about Deadeye. He's pretty unpopular, even with other criminals, because he uses guns. In many ways the whole hero/villain thing is kind of a game, like with the mask thing. So using guns is sort of cheating as far as most of us are concerned. It's fine for normal henchmen and minions, but it's definitely not cool when it comes to bosses. Either way, the truth is, if somebody wants someone else dead, he's the man to hire.

From what I know, he was special ops in the military, but I don't know what branch or anything more specific. The rumor is that he was part of some kind of experiment the government conducted on its own soldiers. It worked, but it also made him kind of crazy.

Deadeye is an expert at practically everything, and Redhawk's a good rider, but I'm sure Alex is holding back for my sake. So why is it that we're gaining on Deadeye?

As we start to catch up, I notice there seem to be a lot of cars around for this late at night. Then I realize they're starting to surround us. Vehicles of every kind pull up: cars, vans, trucks, more bikes. The hunters have become the prey.

Every side street we pass, more vehicles join the posse escorting us. It's no longer a chase. It's become a parade.

Redhawk gives his bike more gas and I follow close behind him, but our "escort" is quickly closing in. At this point I don't even see a way that we can get out of here, even if we wanted to. It's like we're at the center of a swarm of bees and they're getting closer. So what's going to happen? Are we going to stop somewhere, or are they just going to try to shoot at us from all directions as we drive along?

Deadeye heads for the big suspension bridge, and I notice there are no cars around other than the ones that are closing in on us. Something's happened to the normally heavy

CHRISTOPHER J. VALIN

traffic going across the river, and I'm guessing it isn't a welcome party for Harrier's favorite sidekicks.

Not the good kind of welcome party, anyway.

After speeding up for most of our chase, Deadeye suddenly stops on the bridge and turns to face us on his bike. He climbs off and straightens his skull helmet, then slowly adjusts all of his weapons to make sure they're ready: a staff, a sword, and several sidearms. Plus lots and lots of ammunition. I definitely can't see any way this is going to end well.

We slow down as we approach him, and I notice there are now cars coming from behind Deadeye, driving the wrong way on this side of the bridge. The cars on both sides of us are pulled in close to each other, which fences us in. There must be somewhere between fifty and a hundred vehicles surrounding us now, each with at least a couple of guys getting out. It's hard to tell the exact number with so many stretching out into the dark in both directions.

We're good, but we're not that good.

As Redhawk slowly takes off his helmet and hangs it on his handlebar, he doesn't seem too bothered by the whole situation. As opposed to me feeling like I'm about to pee my pants again. He climbs off his bike and starts walking toward

Deadeye as the ever-growing number of criminals moves in on us.

Now that I have a chance to scope things out, I notice the variety of thugs in the group. Rival gang members who would normally kill each other on sight are walking side-by-side. Low-level costumed villains who I know were in prison are scattered throughout the crowd. Right away I spot Med-Evil in his doctor's getup and zombie makeup. At least I hope it's makeup.

I don't understand why these villains, who are usually willing to take on Harrier and me by themselves, are holding back when they have all this backup.

I follow Redhawk's lead and try not to look too scared. Redhawk keeps his collapsible staff in a sheath under his cape, and he pulls it out and extends it, all in one smooth motion. It almost looks like it appears out of nowhere. I pull out the one he gave me, but it's not quite as smooth because I'm so nervous. I need to practice with this thing for sure.

Deadeye doesn't bother to unholster any of his many guns. Instead, he pulls out his own staff and extends it to its full length. Because his mask completely covers his face, I have no idea what expression he has. But I have a feeling it's a smile.

He holds up his hand, and the mob of bad guys stops closing in on us, forming a circle that looks almost like a human arena.

Redhawk doesn't look at me, but he speaks just loud enough for me to hear him. "I want you to hang back and let me take care of this. If you see a chance to escape, take it."

"But——"

"Just listen to me. Please. I don't need your death on my conscience." I step back as Redhawk gets within striking range of Deadeye.

Deadeye is the best assassin in the country. Maybe the world. He's an expert marksman, and as dangerous as Harrier at hand-to-hand combat. Actually more, when you consider the weapons he uses and his lack of a "no killing" rule.

Redhawk is almost as good as Harrier. But somehow I don't think "almost" is going to cut it. He shows off some of his fancy moves——another one of his tactics to distract his enemies——spinning his staff around his body and over his head. Deadeye just stands like a statue and watches him, ready to strike.

In the middle of what looks like an ordinary spinning technique, Redhawk swings his staff directly at Deadeye with what should be a surprise move. Deadeye moves so fast to block it that it's almost too quick for me to follow. Then he strikes back immediately, hitting Redhawk across the jaw.

Redhawk is obviously stunned, but he shakes it off right away and ducks before Deadeye's next swing can catch him on the side of the head. Then he jumps up as Deadeye's next swipe tries to take out his legs.

Instead of coming straight down, Redhawk uses his staff almost like a pole vault and lands his first blow, a kick to Deadeye's chest. This was the assassin's turn to be surprised, and he stumbles back a couple of steps but manages to stay on his feet. As Redhawk comes back down, he uses his body's momentum to swing his staff over his head and come down hard on Deadeye's head. It seems to ring his helmet somewhat, but doesn't do much in the way of damage.

Deadeye comes back with a jab to Redhawk's chest with the end of his staff, but Redhawk's Kevlar body armor takes the brunt of it. It turns out to be just a diversion anyway, as Deadeye's foot shoots out and lands a smack across Redhawk's face that cracks the lenses on his mask and knocks him back to the ground. He follows up with another swing of his staff, and this one makes contact with Redhawk's knee.

Redhawk manages to flip backwards and up onto his feet just before Deadeye can land another blow with his staff. He pulls off his cracked lenses so they don't interfere with his vision and tries to catch his breath for a moment.

I start to move forward, but Redhawk holds up his hand immediately and gives me a warning look. He gets his second wind and goes on the attack, getting in several hits that Deadeye barely has time to block. He swings down hard from above, and when Deadeye blocks it, the assassin's staff shatters.

Deadeye isn't the type of person you want to make look bad in front of all these people. He unsheathes his sword and goes after Redhawk mercilessly. Even though Redhawk is able to avoid any serious wounds, Deadeye does cut him a few times, and the blood is starting to flow pretty heavily.

They continue to dance around one another, but Deadeye continues to cut Redhawk more and more, while Redhawk lands fewer and fewer hits in return. It's obvious that he won't be able to keep up much longer at this rate.

Redhawk knows he won't be able to beat Deadeye in this condition, and uses his staff to vault up into the crowd of bad guys. Using their shoulders and heads, he jumps and flips parkour-style until he's on the railing at the edge of the bridge.

He's holding his side, where there's a pretty deep gash in his uniform.

Some of the thugs in the crowd start reaching for him, but he knows just what to say. "What's the matter, you don't think Deadeye can finish me off himself? He needs help from you losers?"

Redhawk turns and looks me in the eye, and I know exactly what his look is trying to tell me: *Don't let this be in vain.* I hear a shot ring out, and with a jerk, Redhawk goes over the edge of the bridge. I almost scream "No!" like they do in the movies, but then I realize how stupid that would be. I need to escape, and drawing attention to myself like that wouldn't make any sense.

I turn to see Deadeye holding his smoking pistol up, but he's shaking and breathing hard from his battle with Redhawk. He may not be badly wounded, but he's at least winded, which might give me just barely the edge I need.

The criminals are all either looking over the side to see Redhawk hit the water, or cheering and slapping each other on the back. Now's my chance.

I can't just get to the suspension part of the bridge up above——I'll still be surrounded, and Deadeye will have no trouble picking me off. I need to get as far away as possible, fast, while he's distracted. Unfortunately, we're almost to the middle of the bridge, so nothing else is close by.

I shoot my grappler away from the bridge, but I'm too far away from any buildings, and it retracts without hitting anything. I run back toward the beginning of the bridge, but there are a bunch of guys in my way. I start fighting them one by one, thinking about how confident I was just a few weeks ago in that alley. How many could I take down if I had to? This time it's like an endless supply.

I don't have any trouble with the average jerks, but some of the costumed villains are a problem. Music Master, a skinny dude with long red hair sticking out of the top of his mask, hits a chord on his keyboard thing and the sound gives me vertigo and causes me to lose my balance. Creeping Death, an emaciated old guy in a torn-up old spider costume, throws one of his smoke bombs at me and the stench makes me choke. Then one of the few women here, a hot babe in a skimpy costume who calls herself Sensation, uses her light tech to blind me.

I need to try my grappler again because I won't be able to fight like this, but I'm still not sure if I'm close enough.

I point my grappler and shoot and, as it extends as far as it can go, it barely catches the closest building. I hit the button to be reeled in, and a bunch of thugs try to grab me as I go over their heads. Despite everything, I feel myself laugh a little as I zip up out of their reach and head away to someplace safer. I must be a little delirious. I'm only about twenty feet off the ground, but that should be enough to get me to safety before——

CRACK! I hear another shot ring out, and my line goes slack. I know immediately that Deadeye severed it with a bullet.

As I feel myself plummet toward the ground, everything feels like it's moving super slow and I think, *What a stupid way to die after everything I've been through.*

The instant I feel my back hitting the ground, everything goes black.

SEVEN

Beep.

I wake up to an annoying beeping sound and an even more annoying song being sung by the brat. But I'm in strange surroundings, including a bed that's way too comfortable to be my own.

And I have a stabbing pain in my... well, everything. But, hey, on the bright side it looks like my cold is actually gone.

As my eyes focus, I see my mom staring at me with a worried look. "Thank God you're awake. They were afraid that with such a serious head injury you might be out for a long time."

"Head injury?" I look around at my hospital room. Yeah, about what I'd expect with the sorry government health insurance we have. At least nobody is in the other bed next to me.

"It's a good thing your friend was there to call the ambulance for you, or you might not have made it."

Did Alex survive?

"Friend? What frien——" Mom moves aside and I see a girl standing behind her giving me a small wave. I have no idea who she is, but she's cute. With those glasses she has kind of a sexy gamer vibe going on. The kind of girl who can destroy you in Call of Duty and you still want to make out with her later. She seems really shy, though.

"She's like your guardian angel." Mom smiles at her.

"Yep, that's me. I watch him like a hawk." That voice. It can't be. It is. Who else could it be?

"Thanks. I guess I owe you one."

"Yeah. *Another* one, actually." She is not what I expected Osprey to be like in her civilian identity. But, then again, most people would probably say the same thing about me.

I feel bad that I led her on about visiting The Aerie. Or maybe the reason she was watching me in the first place was to try to follow me there. Even so, I can't stay mad at her now.

Mom's look and voice change now that she's not so worried about me. "Then there's the matter of why you were out when you're sick and grounded. The first time I trust you in weeks, and you blow it. And what the hell were you doing skateboarding without a helmet?"

"Skateboarding?" Mom starts to look suspicious at me not knowing what she's talking about.

From behind her, Osprey gives me a warning look. "Must have lost your memory. You know...because of the head injury. It's a good thing you wiped out into that pile of garbage, or it could have been even worse."

"Uh... yeah, I must have. I actually don't remember anything from before my accident." I squint at her. "In fact, I don't remember you being there at all. I do remember another friend being with me. Do you know what happened to him?"

Osprey gets a sad look. "I haven't heard anything. Sorry."

I don't know how Redhawk could have possibly survived that fall, especially with his injuries. But I can't worry about that right now.

Mom is looking at us like we're crazy, and then she gets kind of bitchy with me. "Anyway, when you get out we're going to have a long talk about why you didn't follow the rules. And what kind of additional punishments we're going to have to add."

Osprey looks uncomfortable about the way my mom is talking to me. I'm not sure if she doesn't like it, or if she just thinks it's weird that mom's acting that way in front of her.

"Well, now that I know you're going to be okay, I think I'll get going." She seems pretty nervous for some reason. Something more than just not liking the way my mom is talking to me.

My mom grabs her arm. "I was just about to get a diet soda. I'll walk you out." She turns to the brat. "You stay here with Sawyer for a minute. If you're good, I'll bring you back a candy bar."

The kid nods excitedly. Just what he needs: more sugar. My mom and Osprey leave the room, and the kid stares at the beeping machines. I try to tune him out as he starts singing his song again.

So Osprey was watching me again. She not only saved me, but she showed up in her civilian identity to check on me. Despite my pain, I can't help a big smile. Maybe she isn't just using me to meet Harrier. Maybe she's actually a little bit interested in me for me.

The kid reaches up to one of my monitors like he's going to press a button or something. Leave it to that brat to ruin my moment. "Don't touch that."

He gives me the look he always has when I reprimand him, then flops down into his chair with his arms crossed. My mom pretty much gives him the run of the apartment, so I end up being the disciplinarian a lot of the time. Yet another reason why we don't like each other.

"Your mom was really sad when you were asleep."

"Was she?"

"Yeah. She kept crying and crying and crying."

"I didn't realize that." For the first time, I wonder what she would do if I actually got killed fighting criminals. It never seemed like I was important to her before, but things have changed a lot lately.

"It's a good thing the funny man was here with us to make her happy."

"Funny man?" I try to picture everyone my mom knows. Old boyfriends, neighbors... none of them were very funny. Even in my grogginess, I know something isn't right.

"You know. The clown."

I feel the blood rush out of my face. "There...was a clown here?" I hear the beeping get faster on the machine.

"He was super nice, too."

"What did he look like?"

"I don't know. A big, fat clown."

"Okay, okay. But——"

"He even gave me this." The kid reaches under his chair and pulls out the gift from the funny clown man.

A red kite.

I jolt upright in bed and the vitals monitor starts going crazy. My heart rate speeds up so much it sets off the alarms. I pull the IVs out of my arms and try to stand up, knocking over the IV pole in the process.

My head is swimming and I have tunnel vision as I hear doctors and nurses running down the hall outside. I slam against the doorjamb as I try to exit the room. Mom and Osprey turn around at the end of the hallway and are running back to me just as everything starts to spin.

Then I black out.

✳ ✳ ✳

The next time I wake up, I'm in less pain, but I'm more heavily medicated. It's the middle of the night, and my room is so dark that I can't see anything until my eyes start to adjust in the dim light from the machines. I try to lift my arms and discover I'm strapped down to the bed. They must not want me trying to leave again.

I nearly have a heart attack when I suddenly hear a voice in the darkness at the end of my bed.

"Sawyer William Vincent." I can just barely make out the outline of a figure who appears to be looking at my chart. A very large, very round figure. "You know what that sounds like to me? It sounds like a backwards name."

"What do you want?"

"Oh, I'm merely checking up on you. I have to make sure the doctors do a good job of patching you up for the big finale."

"The what?" I struggle against the restraints, but there's no way I'm getting loose all drugged up this way.

"The climax of the story. The big confrontation. It certainly won't be very fun if you aren't in superb fighting condition."

"Why not just kill me now?"

"That wouldn't do. That wouldn't do at all." I can make out that he's shaking his head vigorously. "You see, I'm going to kill you in front of Harrier like I did his last little boy toy. And then I'm going to finally put him out of his considerable misery."

"What have you done with him?"

"You'll see, child. You'll see. Once you're up and about, come to this address." He pulls out a small card, then lifts up the end of my blankets. He starts to place the card between my toes, then suddenly makes a slicing motion and gives me a giant paper cut. "Oopsie."

He places the card between my toes, pushing it into the paper cut. I grit my teeth but refuse to give him the satisfaction of anything else.

"Oh, and do make sure you're by yourself, little birdie. I'd hate for something horrible to happen to that pretty mommy of yours." He covers my feet back up and then pats them a couple of times.

The figure walks to the door, and when he opens it I can see his wide back in the light from the hall. He's dressed like a doctor. He stops before going all the way out, but doesn't turn around.

"Although... If you wanted to bring your little girlfriend, I suppose I would allow that. I would very much enjoy seeing her again."

He slowly closes the door behind him. I struggle against the restraints, knowing full well I'll never get out of them in my condition.

Then I spend the next few hours wondering how I'm ever going to get through this, until I can't fight the drugs in my system and drift off into some of the worst nightmares I've ever had.

* * *

In my dreams, I'm an actual bird—-some kind of hawk, probably a kite, I guess—-and I'm flying around looking for something. Then I spot an injured black harrier attempting to take flight from its nest on the ground next to a river, but it's unable to stay in the air.

I start to swoop down to help, but then a white osprey catches my attention and I fly off after her. Maybe it's mating season or something. I don't know, you know how dreams are.

When I remember the harrier, I turn and fly back towards it, but before I can get there, an alligator jumps out of the river and chomps it in half in its jaws. The alligator turns, and I see that it has a white face. It seems to grin at me, its teeth full of black feathers.

I wake up and try to figure out why I would have a dream that was so on-the-nose for my situation. My brain is trying to tell me something, but all this medication is messing things up. Is Osprey a distraction, keeping me from finding Harrier? Or is she really someone who can help?

* * *

The next few days in the hospital are excruciating. I'm either lying in bed by myself with my head spinning, trying to figure out my plan for saving Harrier and defeating Pierrot, or I'm putting on a show for my mom, pretending that everything is okay and I can't wait to go home. Even worse, the kid brings the red kite with him every time they visit, reminding me of my situation.

Meanwhile, the crime spree continues to worsen on the streets, and now that I know Pierrot is behind it, the signs are everywhere. Gangs of criminals are now wandering the streets, doing whatever they want to, and ordinary people are hiding in their homes at night. The cops are either too overwhelmed or too scared to put a dent in the situation.

I do have one break in my misery when Fabiola shows up to visit me. Not something I was expecting at all, but I'm definitely not going to complain. I don't even know how she heard about me being in the hospital.

"I heard your accident was bad, but holy crap." She touches the bruises on my face lightly.

"It's not as bad as it looks."

She runs her fingers along the straps holding me down. "What's this all about? Are they afraid you're going to fall out of bed?"

"I tried to walk out of here when I first woke up. You know, 'cause of all the drugs they have me on. So now they keep me strapped down to make sure I don't try it again."

For some reason she really likes hearing this. "That's intense. So you can't move at all?" She leans over me, and her hair brushes against me.

"Not really."

"I hope this doesn't mean you aren't coming to my masquerade party. Are you going to be out by then?"

"I'm not really sure when they're releasing me."

"Well, don't worry. I'm wearing a naughty nurse costume, so even if you're still hurt, I'll take care of you if you show up."

This is so bizarre that I start to think maybe I'm just having another weird dream because of the medication. The thing is, I don't even like this girl. She never even said hi to me before I was on the wrestling team. I mean, yeah, she's really hot, but her IQ is probably lower than her bra size.

"Well, I should let you get some rest. Get better quickly. I don't want you to miss out on the fun." Then she leans down and kisses me on the lips. A real kiss.

My first real kiss.

Maybe things are actually going to start getting better for me. Yeah, except for being in the hospital, having my mentor kidnapped by a homicidal maniac, and getting ready to confront that same maniac on what is probably the most dangerous mission of my life, things are really looking up.

Fabiola turns to leave, and there's Osprey standing in the doorway. To say she looks surprised would be a major understatement. Fabiola looks at Osprey, then back at me, then leaves the room with a little wave in my direction.

Osprey finally shows up so we can talk, and it has to be right now. At the worst possible time. She acts a little cold toward me. That can't be jealousy, can it?

As cute as she is, I still have a hard time imagining her as the same person I was fighting criminals with. She's a little bit skater-girl, maybe a little goth, but mostly kind of nerdy, and definitely not someone you'd think of as a costumed crime fighter.

Then I realize that must be how people see me. To most of the people at school who even notice me, I must seem like some quiet loser without any friends. Except maybe Javier. I should be nicer to him. He really is a good kid, and I can't blame him for wanting to be friends with the only person at school who's nice to him.

And if you add the fact that a lot of the other students blame me for sidelining the quarterback for a few weeks, they probably don't like me very much either.

But isn't that what I want? Isn't that exactly what someone like me or Osprey looks for in a secret identity? Then why do I feel so bummed about it right now?

Probably because, unlike with Fabiola, right now I can picture Osprey and me as normal teenagers who are boyfriend and girlfriend. Hanging out, playing video games, going out for burgers. Whatever "normal" teenagers do. Except for the fact that I don't even know her real name.

"So, now that you know who I really am, are you going to tell me your name?"

"No." She says it so matter-of-factly, as if she's answered the question a billion times.

"Why not?"

"You won't let me into your world. Why should I allow you into mine?"

Ouch. Good point. "Okay. I guess I deserve that."

"Let's be honest. The only reason you've been stringing me along is to get into my pants——tights, whatever. Until you're ready to introduce me to Harrier—or ask me to help you find him—it's going to be strictly professional."

I consider denying it all, but I'm afraid it will just make things worse. Because then I'd be lying to her, and she'd know it.

"I would like your help. Especially now that Redhawk is gone. He believed Harrier's disappearance was because he was investigating Pierrot, even though he's supposed to be dead."

"Do you think someone is getting some sort of revenge for Pierrot?"

I hesitate to tell her the truth. I still don't know her very well, and I really don't know how much I can trust her.

"We weren't able to find much out at all. From the computer or informants."

"You don't think Pierrot could still be alive, do you?"

I calculate the risks of telling her versus the help she could provide, and decide to let her know everything.

"From what I know about the explosion that he was supposedly killed in, I wouldn't have thought it was possible. But something really strange happened to me."

I explain to her what happened to me the night Pierrot gave me the card. She tells me about the day the clown showed up in my room when I was unconscious, and about the creepy way he kept staring at her.

I show her the card he left, with the address written on the back, along with tomorrow's date and a time: 9:00 p.m. "I have to go there."

"Don't you think it's a trap?"

"Of course it's a trap. And Pierrot knows I know it's a trap. But he also knows I'll go anyway."

"You can't."

"I have to. Harrier will die. If he isn't dead already."

"I'm going with you."

"No. No way. It's way too dangerous."

"So it makes more sense for you to go alone?" I've never seen her this serious before.

"I can't put you in that kind of danger."

"You're not 'putting me' into anything. I'm making my own decision."

"But I can't——"

"Look: I don't want to embarrass you, but I'm actually older than you, and, unlike you, technically an adult. I'm going to go with you whether you like it or not, and I don't think there's a whole lot you can do about it."

I sigh. She's right. This is a woman who, without any assistance, became a crime fighter just by making her own costume and training herself to be a great martial artist. Who am I to tell her what she can or can't do?

Besides, I don't think I can even get out of this bed without her help.

* * *

Osprey and I set up a plan for me to sneak out of the hospital just after the nurse comes by during her rounds the next night. She already went by and checked out the address, which is some old warehouse down at the docks. Now we just have to figure out a way to get me there in time for my little meeting with Pierrot.

First she loosens the restraints that have been holding me down. Then she has to go back to my place and basically break in to get my spare costume, because she dumped the one I had been wearing somewhere along the way when she brought me to the hospital. I'm not sure what I was wearing when I got here, but I don't ask her because I don't really want to know the answer. Chances are she got the clothes off of a homeless guy or out of a dumpster.

It's really uncomfortable to think about her going in through my bedroom window—-which I have rigged to be able to get into from the outside with a special trick and a screwdriver—-and going through my stuff. It's not like I was expecting to have her over and cleaned up my room beforehand or anything. I just hope she doesn't do any snooping other than just looking for the costume and getting out. That could end up being really awkward. I have to force myself to stop going through the list of things she might come across that would make me want to die.

At least Mom didn't throw out the spare costume or give it away, even though she thinks I paid for it with money from selling drugs. But this is the old version, without the attached grappler, the glider cape and the jets.

And no mints in the utility belt. Maybe I can stop by the hospital gift shop on the way out.

After the nurse leaves my room, I pull one hand loose from the restraints, then free myself. At least the IVs are out of my arms now. I hop out of bed and—-whoa, that's not good. It's been too long since I stood up, and I'm pretty shaky here.

I'm sure the hospital food, with all that Jell-o and broth, isn't helping much either. I wonder if I have time to stop for a burger on my way to that warehouse.

I look at the clock. Damn. The nurse was running late on her rounds, and now I have to rush to get over to that address in time. I have no idea what will happen if I don't make the meeting, but from what I've heard about Pierrot, I shouldn't take a chance on finding out.

My legs are so wobbly that I feel like I'm walking on noodles. How am I ever going to do this?

I crack open the door to my room and peek out to assess the situation. A couple of orderlies are talking down at one end of the hall, and a doctor is going through some paperwork down at the other. When the doctor turns around, I sneak out and head in that direction, then slip into the first non-patient room I come across. It's some kind of locker room, and I thought it was empty at first, but then I notice a doctor asleep on a cot in the corner.

I'm going to need to get out of this hospital gown if I'm going to get out of here without drawing attention to myself. I check a couple of the lockers, but it looks like they're all locked. After looking around for a minute, I find a couple of paper clips lying around and pick the lock on one of the lockers. There are scrubs inside, but they're pink. I need to try another one.

Damn, that doctor is waking up. No time to be picky about the color. I pull on the pants quickly and strip off the gown. Since Dr. Sleepyhead is sitting up now, I pull the scrub shirt over my head as I exit the room, hoping nobody is standing right outside to see me.

The scrubs are both too big and too short for me at the same time, and I look completely ridiculous. If anything, I'll probably draw more attention to myself than I would have wearing the gown.

I manage to make it down to the end of the hallway, but just as I start to open the door to the stairwell, I see my nurse come out of my room. Why was she back in there?

She looks down the hall in both directions, and spots me just as I'm going through the door. Great. Now security is going to be after me. Why are they treating me like a criminal?

I head down the stairs as fast as my noodle legs will carry me, which isn't very fast at all. Up above, I can hear a couple of security guys talking as they rush down the stairs, so I know I don't have a lot of time.

Just then, I see Osprey on her way up to meet me, still in her civilian clothes. Before I can say anything, she rushes past me, dropping a duffel bag. A couple of flights up, the security guys shout in surprise, then make some unpleasant noises just before being knocked unconscious.

Osprey comes back down to join me and picks up the bag. I try to give her a stern look.

"I was hoping to avoid hurting anyone here at the hospital."

"Couldn't be helped. And you're welcome."

We exit the stairwell at the bottom of the stairs near the lobby. A bunch of security guards have gathered there, knowing it's my only way out.

Osprey looks at the guards, then at me. "You ready for a fight?"

"No. And I said I don't want to hurt anyone."

She grabs me around the waist and pulls her grappling gun out of the bag. "Then I guess we'll have to improvise."

She shoots her grappler at the front doors of the hospital just as someone is walking in. The hook flies past the person and connects with a pole just outside the doors. When she hits the button to retract the line, we start to slide through the lobby fast. The guards try to grab us, but they end up running into each other like they're in an old-fashioned comedy film.

Just as we're about to go through the doorway, I notice a kid standing by the door holding a Happy Meal. I grab it out of his hand. "Sorry!"

I immediately feel guilty about taking the kid's food, but it had to be done. Sometimes stuff happens when you're working for the greater good.

As soon as we're out the door, Osprey disconnects the grappler again and shoots it up to a nearby rooftop. Before anyone can even follow us out, we're gone.

Once we're safely on a roof nearby, I open up the box. "Dammit!"

Osprey looks worried. "What is it? What's wrong?"

"Nuggets. I was so craving a burger. Even a crappy one. And look at this! Apple slices! I don't even get fries."

"You poor baby. Maybe we can stop——"

"No. There's no time. I'm not even sure we're going to get there in time as it is." I scarf down the food and get my costume on as quickly as I can. It fits kind of snug since it was made a couple of years ago, and the design is a little bit different ·

from the newer one. It also doesn't offer as much protection because it doesn't have some of the newer pieces of armor attached to it.

It's also missing the glider cape.

I try not to gawk as Osprey changes into her own costume, but it's really difficult.

I'm probably going to be dead within the next couple of hours anyway, what do I have to lose? I sneak a peek, and she immediately busts me.

"Eyes forward, soldier."

"Sorry. It's... You know." My face must be redder than my costume right now.

She smiles. "It's okay. I know how irresistible I am." She finishes pulling on her costume and walks over to me. "Don't worry about it. I had to strip you down before I took you to the hospital, so now we're even."

She's standing so close to me that I can feel her breath. I should try to kiss her. What difference will it make? I'm going on a suicide mission. I start to lean forward.

But what if she doesn't want me to? Is she giving me a signal right now? How do I know? Why am I such a geek? I think she wants me to. I'm going to go for it. But what if she doesn't?

She leans in and gives me a small kiss. On the lips. The lips! But then she pulls away. What does that mean? Was that a real kiss? Or a "hope you don't die" kiss? Or an "okay, I feel sorry for you" kiss? Maybe her seeing Fabiola kissing me wasn't so bad after all.

I don't have time for this! "We better get going."

She isn't happy taking orders. "Yes, *sir.*"

"Look, if Pierrot is as insane as I've heard, I'm not interested in finding out what happens if I'm late."

We take off across the rooftops in the direction of the warehouse, but Osprey still wants to talk. "You don't really think he'd kill him, would he? I mean, he's had him for weeks. Why would he all of a sudden kill him now?"

"Maybe you missed the part where I said he's insane." That came out harsher than it should have. I should be happy about the kiss. Why does it seem like I'm upset about it?

"It just seems like he went through a lot of trouble to capture Harrier and lure you there...even keeping you alive when he could have had you killed, or even killed you himself. Even for a crazy person, that doesn't make any sense."

"He's punishing Harrier, and I'm somehow part of that plan. I just don't know what part." Actually, I do, assuming he was telling me the truth. He wants to kill me in front of Harrier to torture him. He knows Harrier will blame himself for getting another kid involved after what happened to the last one.

But I can't let Osprey know any of that.

As we run across the roof of one of the nicer buildings in the neighborhood, I hear loud music playing across the street and a bunch of teenagers talking really loud. It sounds like there's some kind of fight going on. If only that was it.

Even though I tell myself to stay out of it and focus, I still glance down to check out what's happening. In a coincidence I wouldn't believe if I saw it in a movie or TV show, it turns out to be Fabiola's party. The biggest event of the school year. And I'm missing it.

But the noise isn't because of a fight, like I thought it was. Someone dressed in a Black Harrier costume is shoving someone dressed like...me? And the Red Raptor guy isn't fighting back. A group of teenagers in other costumes starts to surround the smaller kid.

I know I'm repeating myself when I say I don't have time for this. But something tells me I better make time.

As I listen carefully, I recognize "Harrier's" voice. Of course it's Logan. Who else? But what really surprises me is the voice of "Raptor." It's actually Javier.

"I'm sorry. I'll leave."

"Not until I'm done with you, loser. The only reason we invited you was to get your idiot friend to come."

"He's in the hospital."

"I know, you stupid moron. So why did you bother to show up?"

I attach my rope to a drainpipe and rappel down the side of the building just as Osprey notices I'm not keeping up with her. She glides down after me. "What are you doing?"

"I have to."

I get closer and see Fabiola come out with her naughty nurse outfit on. It's a big relief, since I'm sure she'll put a stop to it and I won't have to step in.

She grabs Logan's arm. "Just hit him and get it over with. I can't believe he had the nerve to come to my house."

Wow, was I ever wrong.

Just as Logan cocks his fist back, I manage to get between them. He gives me a strange look. "Who the hell are you?"

"I'm the *real* Red Raptor."

"He's called 'Red Kite' you freaking 'tard."

I look at Osprey and she smiles as she says, "I know, I know, you don't have time for this."

I haul off and hit Logan square in the face. Even in my weakened state, it's plenty hard enough to knock him unconscious. There are a hundred other ways I could have taken him down, some of them without hurting him. But that just wouldn't have felt right.

Fabiola rushes to his side and lifts up his head. "Logan! Logan?" She stands up and shoves me as hard as she can and then gets in my face.

"What did you do to him? How did you——?" She stops and tilts her head. She squints at me and I can tell that a hint of recognition is starting to form.

POW! Osprey knocks her on her ass with one punch.

Osprey gives me a crooked grin. "Well, I knew *you* weren't going to do it."

The rest of the crowd backs away, afraid to mess with us.

We turn to leave, and Javier calls after us. "Hey!" I turn around for a second, to give him a chance to thank me.

"That's Kite's old costume, you know. You really should update it."

I can't even catch a break after saving someone's ass.

But his comment does make me realize that I had transferred most of my tools and weapons to my new utility belt when I got it, which means I only have basic stuff with me on my most dangerous mission ever. I look down at my old, slightly faded backup threads, then turn to Osprey. "Are you sure you don't remember where you dumped my good costume?"

* * *

We finally arrive at the address, and I start thinking I'm actually going to be on time for my "appointment". Then I realize there doesn't seem to be any way in. The place is huge—like an airplane hangar—and scary as hell on the outside. It's almost like someone dressed the place up for a Halloween party, or to be a haunted house. In fact, I'm not even sure how much of the painting on the outside is Pierrot's work and how much is just graffiti.

We circle the perimeter, and sure enough there are no doors, and all of the windows are welded completely shut.

Osprey suggests we head up to the roof as I start to panic about what's going to happen as Pierrot's deadline passes.

Up on the roof, we have the same problem. No doors, no skylights, no way in at all. The entire area is covered in junk and stupid horror stuff, as if someone put up Halloween decorations years ago and never bothered to take them down. Just as I'm about to give up, Osprey notices a small hatch in the far corner, hidden in some debris. She also figures out how to open it, since it's not obvious just from looking at it.

As we open it up and start the climb down into who knows what, I realize I probably never would have made it here without her help.

EIGHT

Explosions.

Really cool and fun in an action movie. Not so much up close in real life. It's just one of the traps the Pierrot has waiting for us when we get inside. If he wanted to kill me, he could have done it a bunch of times by now. He could have sliced my throat in the hospital. Deadeye could have shot me instead of killing Weasel. The entire mob of bad guys could have converged on me on the bridge and taken me down with the sheer force of numbers.

It's the same with all the explosions that keep going off. None of them are big enough or close enough to kill me, but they do make me dizzy and knock out my hearing for a while. They have me completely on edge. Never deadly, though.

Probably not even loud enough to bring the cops, if he has as much soundproofing as I imagine he does.

So I go in knowing that he doesn't want me dead——yet——but I still have to worry about what kind of shape I'll be in by the time I reach him. It's like when the biggest, toughest gang member hangs back while the others soften me up.

And I have to worry about Osprey's safety. I'm sure Pierrot probably knows that Harrier doesn't care about her, so the only reason for him to allow her to come with me would be to hurt or kill her in front of me to demoralize me further. Just one in a long list of reasons why I should have figured out a way to prevent her from joining me.

He has the entire warehouse set up in some sort of maze, with everything in it meant to disorient me. Hallways shrink and then widen, then turn back on themselves. There are big mirrors everywhere to make things more confusing, and in addition to the explosions, loud music coming from hidden speakers. Every fifty yards or so, there's a big flat screen TV with the sound blasting over the music. Right now they're playing recorded news stories about how Harrier hasn't been seen in so long. Another tactic to throw me off, I guess. Note to self: add an earplug compartment to the utility belt.

I turn to Osprey. "Stay close. The last thing we need is to get separated in this madhouse."

"Oh, you don't have to worry about that. I have to admit, I'm pretty much terrified."

At one point, the hallway narrows until it's nothing more than a crawlspace. In fact, he probably just led us up into the actual crawlspace of the building now that I think about it. It's really dark except for the TV screen up ahead. Pierrot's face suddenly fills the screen.

"Welcome to my funhouse, birdie. Or is it dinosaur now? I'm so confused. We're going to have *so*. Much. Fun. But first, I suppose you'll be wanting to see how Harrier's doing at some point. Well, no time like the present." Pierrot steps back from the camera and I can see Harrier in the background.

It's horrible.

Harrier and I have been in bad shape before after some really intense fights, but nothing has ever prepared me for this. His uniform, except for his mask, is almost completely gone, and what's left of it is hanging in tatters from his bruised, bloody body. He's hanging from chains that are cuffed around his wrists, and he's covered in cuts from head to toe. He's obviously been tortured.

I must have let out some kind of sound when I first saw him, but I can't tell you what it was. I feel the anger well up inside of me after the shock wears off. I can't wait to get my hands on that evil bastard. He won't know what hit him.

"Oh, and by the way——this is for you being late." He reaches for something off-screen, and suddenly an electric jolt zaps Osprey and me. Not too much, but I've been hit with a Taser before, and it was along those lines.

I whisper to Osprey. "Glad you came along?"

"I'll be fine. We need to save him." She looks back at the screen again. I'm going to have to force myself not to think about the torture Harrier's been through while he's been here. If I dwell on it too much, it's going to throw me off my game and put all of us in even more danger.

While Osprey and I are focused on Harrier, a hidden trap door opens under her all of a sudden, and then immediately closes up again after she falls through. I hear her start to scream, but it cuts off as soon as it closes. I have no idea how far she fell, or what she landed on at the bottom of the drop. For all I know, I may have just watched her die.

What if she is dead? I don't even know her name. I wouldn't be able to tell her family. Does she even have a family?

Would she just end up as another girl who goes missing and nobody ever finds out what happened to her?

I try desperately to pull open the trap door with my fingers, but I can't get a grip around the edges. I grab one of my throwing stars to see if I can force it open, but I don't have any luck with that either. In desperation, I start pounding on it, but I realize it's not going to help anything. So I continue to crawl through, determined to get through the maze as quickly as possible so I can save Harrier, and hopefully now Osprey also.

The crawlspace ends by opening up into a dark room that appears empty from what I can tell. I lower myself down to the floor, which is about twelve feet down. I feel around with my foot, allowing my eyes to adjust to the darkness. Normally I'd use my light, but I don't want to give away my position to anyone—-or anything—-that might be lurking in here.

Just as I start to be able to make out where I'm going and I reach the center of the room, bright lights suddenly come on from all directions, blinding me now that my pupils have fully dilated. At the same time, loud music blasts from giant speakers embedded in the walls in a grid pattern.

I shut my eyes, cover my ears, and fall to my knees. Why is Pierrot doing this? Why not either kill me now or let me get to where he's keeping Harrier so he can kill me then? Is he somehow making Harrier watch this, assuming it will torture him? From what I saw on that video screen, it's hard to imagine Harrier being able to focus on anything right now.

Even with my ears covered, the sound is so deafening that I can't think straight. I open my eyes and see Music Master standing several yards away, playing his keyboard device. His music isn't the only thing loud about him. His stupid, colorful costume and bright orange hair hurt my eyes just looking at them.

Obviously, he's controlling the sound, so if I can take him out, it should stop. I look around the room, but it's empty except for the speakers and the lights in the walls. I try to stand, but the sound is causing me to have vertigo, and I fall back down. I also feel nauseous. Great...puking is going to end up becoming my signature move.

I remember that I have earplugs in my utility belt, but as I reach for them, I realize they're in my new utility belt—the one that Osprey dumped off somewhere. I need to appreciate my new gadgets a lot more. If I live through this, anyway.

I can't concentrate enough to hit him or his keyboard with my throwing stars. If only there was some way of reaching him from here. I can't even crawl over to him.

Then I remember Osprey's solution to reaching the door at the hospital.

I pull my old grappler off my belt, and Music Master's expression quickly goes from joy to curiosity. Then it changes to realization a second too late as I shoot the hook at him and it attaches to his keyboard, which is strapped around him. The sound stops immediately.

I brace myself and retract the cable, and because he wasn't ready for it, he's pulled toward me extremely fast. Just as he's about to reach me, I do a flying kick and allow the grappler to launch me toward Music Master as he continues moving in my direction. The kick nearly takes his head off, and he drops to the ground like a sack of potatoes. I check to make sure I didn't actually kill him, but he seems to just be unconscious.

I unhook the keyboard from its strap and smash it against the wall as hard as I can, even though I know he has many of them and this won't stop him the next time he gets out of jail. It takes everything I have not to smash it over his head.

The bright lights start up again, flashing on and off, getting faster and faster until they produce a strobe effect.

I think I figured out a pattern here. If Music Master created that sound, then obviously the person who created the light show is—-

"Hello, sweetie." I turn around, and Sensation is already behind me. There must be a hidden doorway somewhere in here.

No matter how many times I see her, I can never get over how hot she looks. I've never been to a strip club, but I imagine this must be how the women look before they take their clothes off. Most heroes and villains don't actually have costumes like the ones in the comics. They wear some combination of lightweight body armor, Kevlar, and other microfibers. But Sensation is a major exception, all in spandex and glitter, like she was drawn by a pinup artist.

So, idiot that I am around females, I stand there with my mouth open instead of reacting immediately. That gives her plenty of time to roundhouse kick me in the head, knocking me to the floor. Now my head's throbbing on top of everything else, and I think I strained my neck.

I'm not sure what kind of technology she uses, but she's able to do a lot of things with her light shows. Right now, I feel myself not being able to move very well or to track her with the strobe light flashing. I don't know whether it's a trick of the lights or if I somehow end up with gaps in my perception, but she appears to flash in and out of placcs.

The next thing I know, she's behind me again, this time using a flying kick to hit me in the back and slam me into the wall, breaking the light fixture there. I can feel where the glass cut into my face, and even through parts of my old costume that aren't armored.

I forgot what a good hand-to-hand fighter she is on top of the light show.

I remember what Harrier taught me I should do the next time we fought her, and close my eyes, listening for her footsteps. She's so quiet, I almost don't pick it up, but then I hear an almost imperceptible crunch as she steps on a piece of glass.

I hate hitting a woman—-my mom would kill me if she ever found out—-but I kind of think Sensation deserves it. Oh, man, I hope that doesn't make me sound like some kind of a-hole who makes excuses for abusing his wife or something. I mean, she is helping a homicidal maniac who's trying to kill a teenager, isn't she?

And right now, she's doing a pretty good job of it.

I swing out my leg, and it connects with her stomach. From the sound she makes, I can tell I got her pretty good. I continue my momentum forward and punch for where her face should be, and I'm successful there as well. My next move is to sweep her legs out from under her, and I hear her fall to the ground.

I fall onto her chest and hold my forearm against her windpipe. "Turn it off."

She tries to wriggle out from under me, grunting with effort. Her voice sounds almost like a cartoon duck because of the pressure on her throat. "Get away from me, you little—-"

"I said turn it off!"

Finally she gives in and presses the buttons in her glove or whatever it is that controls her light shows. Now I have to figure out what to do with her. I can't have her showing up when I'm in the middle of my showdown with Pierrot. It's going to be nearly impossible to defeat him as it is.

I pull a zip tie out of my utility belt and tell her to turn around and stay in a seated position. But as I start to bind her hands behind her back, she flips over and gets me into a headlock with her legs.

I can't breathe at all, and I feel myself losing consciousness fast. Things start to go dark with little stars flying around as I feel around for something to hit her with. I manage to grab hold of Music Master's ruined keyboard with my fingertips, and slide it toward me. Just as I feel like it's going to be lights out, I get both hands around the keyboard and smash her in the face with it as hard as I can.

Her leg-lock goes slack as she collapses to the ground. So much for going easy on her.

All I can think about is resting right now, but I have to keep moving. Harrier may not have much time left even if Pierrot doesn't directly kill him, and I don't even want to think about what that clown and his men could be doing to Osprey right now.

After tying both of them up with some zip ties, I use Sensation's cape to wipe the blood from my face and the other parts of my body that are bleeding, and start searching the walls. I manage to locate the doorway in the opposite corner of the room from where I came in, and carefully open it. Inside is a dark, cramped hallway that I have to duck down in to move forward.

This is typical of supervillains in this town. They come up with some hokey plan and think it's clever. First they assault my hearing, then my sight. Next will probably be smell, which makes sense, because the other costumed baddie that was on the bridge along with Music Master and Sensation was Creeping Death.

But who am I going to face when I get to "touch," assuming I live that long? Who else was on the bridge besides...

No. No, no, no, no. There's no way I'm going to be able to face Deadeye in this condition. I wouldn't stand a chance against him alone, even at my peak.

I can't think about it right now. I just have to focus on the moment and worry about dealing with that if and when it comes up.

In the dark hallway, I feel a stickiness on the bottom of my boots, and soon I notice webbing hanging down from the top also. It doesn't get bad enough that I can't move and I know from past experience with Creeping Death that it won't do any good to try to cut it.

I can see up ahead that there's a dim light coming from an opening, and I can already smell some sort of gas. If I had my regular utility belt, I'd be putting on my small breather right now, but this old one doesn't have it. I have to make a decision to either go through quietly and assess the situation, or rush in and try to surprise him. Normally Harrier makes these calls, and I realize I'm not very good at deciding because I haven't had a lot of practice.

I decide to go in head first and fists blazing.

It's hard to get a running start with the stickiness, but I'm going at a pretty good speed when I burst through the opening and roll forward. I get up into a crouch and look around, but I don't see the Creepster anywhere. There's already a haze in the room, making it so I can't see more than a few feet in any direction. The smell is already beginning to burn my nostrils and my lungs.

I turn in circles as quickly as I can without making myself dizzy, hoping to catch him before he can get to me from any direction. Unfortunately, I didn't think about him coming from above like a spider, so when he lands on my shoulders, it's a complete surprise. He grabs the sides of my head and digs his sharp fingernails into me, surprisingly strong for a bony old man.

Luckily, it doesn't take much for me to figure out how to get him off. I move as if I'm going to do a backflip, which ends up slamming his head into the floor hard. I jump away from him to get my bearings, but he drops another one of his gas bombs, and now my lungs feel like they're on fire and he disappears again into the haze.

Okay, think. These crazies always do things according to their theme. What's he going to do next?

Attack from below. I think of it a split second too late as I feel something clamp around both of my ankles. I can't move my feet. They're in some kind of cuffs that are attached to the floor.

I hear Creeping Death's cackling laugh. I don't know if this guys' been smoking two packs a day for fifty years, or if he's just breathed in too much of his own creations, but he sounds like he's going to hack up a lung.

Just like I can never tell whether his old, faded costume is part of his theme, or if he's just too cheap to get a new costume. It looks like it hasn't been washed in my lifetime.

Some kind of whip snaps at me from behind and wraps around my arms so I can't move them. The old man dances around me in circles, wrapping his long whip tighter around me. Between the dancing and the cackling, I'm almost sure he's completely lost it.

There's one idea I had a couple of years ago that Harrier actually gave me a lot of praise for. After constantly being locked up by these costumed villains and not being able to get to our lock picks in our utility belts, I convinced him that we needed to come up with a way to hide them in our gauntlets. Because we wear bracers over our forearms, it wasn't too difficult to hide the tools up there. I squat down before he can get the whip around my legs, and my hands are able to reach the cuffs around my feet. In less than a minute, I'm able to unlock both cuffs without him noticing a thing.

I don't know what Creeping Death's plan is, or if he even has a plan, but it ends now. As soon as he gets to the point where he's directly in front of me, I launch myself forward and barrel into him. He was not ready for that at all.

He drops his whip and I roll in the opposite direction that it's wrapped around me. It finally loosens up to the point where I can take it off of me.

I can't see him through the haze, but I hear him whimper from the ground where he's lying. Probably broke a hip or something.

What? I'm supposed to feel sorry for this guy?

The whip starts to move, so he must be picking it back up. No way I'm letting him have another crack at me. I grab the end of the whip near me and yank on it as hard as I can. I think he's afraid to let go because he'll fall down again, so he's hanging on tight as I see his ratty old spider costume coming at me. I prepare to kick him hard, but at the last second I actually do feel bad.

Instead, I step out of the way and he runs into the nearest wall head first, knocking himself unconscious. Wrapping him up in his own whip to make sure he can't come after me, I decide I better check his pulse to make sure he didn't croak. It's weak, but still there. And, dude, his breath smells worse than his stink bombs.

I search the room completely, and it turns out the only way out is an opening in the ceiling. I silently thank Osprey again for bringing along an extra grappler as I shoot it up into the opening and it attaches to something solid. Rising up above the room, I notice tiny cameras in each corner of the ceiling. I didn't see any in the other rooms, but I didn't get up this high, so I'm sure they were there.

Apparently all of this is part of a show for Pierrot's entertainment.

I climb into the opening in the ceiling and crawl through what feels like another duct. In the complete darkness, I start to notice a slight downward incline, and then it quickly gets steeper. Too late, I realize it's actually moving, and the surface has gone from ordinary metal to something really slick. I start to move faster, and just when I'm about to put my hands out to the sides and stop myself, razor-sharp blades spring out. I pull my limbs in as close to my body as I can so I don't get cut, but that makes me like a bobsledder hurtling down the slide.

As I spot a light up ahead, I prepare myself to be launched into whatever's at the end of this ride.

* * *

The slide dumps me out in a cavernous room filled with tons of old amusement park stuff. There are seats from rides, signs for attractions, animatronic characters, costumes, and lots and lots of junk. And I go crashing through all of it at very high speed.

It's time for the "touch" portion of the program. A giant hand grabs me by the cape and lifts me into the air like a doll. I should have known. La Cucaracha.

I guess Pierrot got him released from jail. Or maybe he just made bail. Either way, he's back in fighting shape. And, with his body odor, he could have easily been the "smell" portion of their plan instead.

I barely have time to be relieved that it wasn't Deadeye I have to deal with when he chuckles as he grabs one of my ankles and lifts me completely above his head.

There's no way I'm defeating this monster in my condition. I might as well just give up now. He throws me through a thin sign, and I roll into another part of the gigantic room. When I come to a stop, I want to lie there and just let him kill me. I'm ready for it to be over with.

But then I see them. Pierrot. Harrier. On the other side of the room. I'm so close to the end. I can't give up now.

La Cucaracha is going to be on top of me any second now. I can hear him grunting as he walks toward me. I feel around in my utility belt, trying to figure out what I might still have in there.

Most of the compartments are empty. Just a few throwing stars, but I know they're worthless against him.

Then I find some pepper spray just in time as he's about to grab me again. I spray it directly into his eyes, and he screams in rage. I'm not sure how much actually got into his eyes, though, because the eyeholes in his mask are pretty small. Either way, I can't believe that with all the high-tech weapons I normally have at my disposal, I took him down with something I can get at a convenience store for a couple of bucks.

I pull out a throwing star and try cutting the tubes again like last time, but it's useless. The new ones are made of some really strong material. I guess he——or, more likely, Pierrot—— wanted to make sure I didn't defeat him the same way again.

I manage to stand up weakly and I grab one of the boards from the broken sign. Maybe I can break the serum bottles that give him his strength. Without the serum, he's not only weak, but he doesn't really know how to fight, so I can take him down easily.

I swing directly at the bottles, but they're also made of something too strong to be affected by it.

Desperate, I try a kick and a punch in a couple of his more vulnerable areas, but he barely notices as he claws at his eyes.

Then he looks directly at me, his eyes bulging and bright red, and grabs me by my shoulders. He lifts me above his head again and tosses me across the room in the direction of Pierrot.

I allow myself to go limp so I don't break anything as I hit the floor and roll once again to a stop. For a second, I feel like I can't move and I'm worried I'm going to be paralyzed. I wiggle my fingers and toes just to make sure I still can.

I look over at Harrier, who's trying to lift his head long enough to see if I'm okay. He manages to get it up for a second, and in that second I manage to get out, "I'm sorry."

La Cucaracha makes it over to me before I can even think about moving yet, and he's still in a rage. He stands above me and, with a roar, lifts his foot for the killing blow. He's going to literally stomp on my head, and I know it's going to smash open like a melon. There's no way I'm surviving this.

BLAM! A shot rings out and La Cucaracha slumps down, falling on top of me. He's so heavy that it's only slightly better than having my head stomped in.

Behind him stands Deadeye, once again holding an actual smoking gun in his hand. Pierrot shoves him to the side as he throws a tantrum about La Cucaracha almost killing me.

"I warned him to stick to the plan. Why is it so difficult for everyone to stick to the plan?" He runs over and kicks La Cucaracha's lifeless body over and over, screaming like a little girl who had her ponytail pulled.

This is the first chance I have to get a good look at Pierrot in person. So much different than in the pictures. So much scarier. Unlike most brightly-colored clown costumes, his is all black and white—-even his makeup. Instead of a red smiley-face, he has a black frown painted on, and tears drawn on his cheeks coming down from the black around his eyes. He's way too overweight to be exerting himself this way, and he starts breathing heavily as the sweat smudges his makeup.

This is not what I was expecting at all.

I try to push La Cucaracha off of me, but he's far too heavy and I'm way too weak. Pierrot finally stops and tries to calm himself down, breathing heavily as if he's just run a race. He snaps his fingers and his two regular henchmen come over and drag La Cucaracha off of me. Then they help me get to my feet.

I thank them both by using my last bit of energy to knock them unconscious with roundhouse kicks to the head.

Pierrot makes a tsk-ing sound. "Now what did you go and do that for? Do you have any idea how hard it is to find good henchmen these days? And let me tell you: their union is a real problem. I can barely afford the overtime anymore."

I'm starting to see why criminals get so annoyed with the witty banter. It's no fun when you're on the other end of it.

Deadeye pulls his Bo staff from its sheath on his back and faces me. I can barely stand and my legs are shaking hard, but I try not to show it. He can probably kill me with one blow——what am I saying? He can *definitely kill me with one blow*. I've been going on adrenaline for too long now, and I don't think there's anything left in me. I've been ignoring my injuries because I'm afraid of what I'll find when I start to check them out. It's like I'm already defeated, and I haven't even gotten to my main enemy yet. I just have to go through the deadliest assassin on earth to get to him.

The only question is whether Pierrot had him shoot La Cucaracha to save me for himself, or whether he wanted Deadeye to have the honor of killing me. Thankfully, I get the answer right away.

"Mr. Deadeye, I believe I have this young man right where I need him at this point. Thank you for all your assistance with my grand plan—-you were absolutely brilliant. Now go take the rest of the evening off."

Deadeye shrugs and puts his staff back. I notice I'm starting to breathe again when I didn't even realize I had been holding my breath. As Deadeye leaves the warehouse, I feel like I've been pardoned from a death sentence. Except the reality is that Pierrot is actually far more dangerous than even Deadeye.

And now it's down to Pierrot and me.

"Release Harrier. Now." With Deadeye gone I get a little bit of confidence back, but I'm mostly faking it because I have nothing else to lose.

"Oh... I see. You think you can just waltz into *my* funhouse and start barking orders. What in the world gave you that idea?"

I move toward him and make it clear with my body language that my intention is to beat him senseless.

"No. Nyet. Non. Nein. Don't step any closer, little bird. Or the girl gets it."

I look around. "What girl?"

He walks over to a fake Egyptian sarcophagus and swings it open. Osprey tumbles out to the floor, her hands tied in front of her. She doesn't look too good.

Pierrot holds Osprey by her hair. Her costume is torn, and her cape is missing. She looks like she's nearly unconscious.

"I'm so glad you brought your girlfriend, little birdie. She's oh-so delicious. Once I'm done with you and Hack Derrier over there, I'm going to have *so* much fun with her." He sticks out his slimy tongue and licks her neck from her collarbone to her ear.

I take a step toward him, but that causes him to yank her head back hard, so I stop. "Let her go. She isn't part of this."

"Isn't part of this? Of course she is. She was always part of the plan. You can't possibly think you met by accident, can you? Think about it. She was there when you needed her. To save you. To push you along. To make sure you got here. Did you think it was all a coincidence?"

He can't be telling the truth. What does he mean? That Osprey was working for him? For Harrier? What?

I go through everything in my mind. She showed up when I was falling, so she was watching me then. She was there when that punk took my picture. And she somehow saved me from that criminal mob and took me to the hospital. Was she a spy for Pierrot that whole time? Moving me toward coming here all along? Or is he just trying to get to me some more and make sure I don't trust anyone?

My expression must give away what I'm thinking, because Osprey speaks even though it seems like it's a huge effort for her. "Not...true."

Pierrot sneers. "Oh, don't be so modest, girl. You were wonderful. Don't denigrate your fantastic performance by pretending it was all real. I'm sure he knows deep down that someone like you would never want anything to do with someone like..." He turns and looks at me in disgust. "...him."

Osprey somehow gets up the strength to lift up her knee and then slam her foot back into his crotch. Pierrot snarls with rage and throws her down to the ground.

I run to her while Pierrot doubles over in pain, holding his junk. He makes a strange groaning noise that is going to keep me awake at night if I ever get a chance to go to bed again after this.

Osprey looks up at me, her eyes pleading. She can barely get her words out through her sobbing. "Please. He's lying. Please don't..."

She passes out. She seems to be okay when I check her pulse and everything. I look back at Harrier to make sure he's still breathing. I'm done with this game. I have to get them both to a hospital right away.

At this point, I don't care who's telling the truth. Pierrot's going to pay for this. All of it.

I wipe the blood from my face as I stand and face Pierrot. The rage continues to build inside of me, and I can feel the adrenaline pumping again. I'm in bad shape myself. Hurt almost as bad as when I was in the hospital. But I'm going to finish this fight. And I'm going to win.

Pierrot holds up his hands. "Hold on. Before you get all punchie-hittie with me, there are some other things I think you're going to be very interested in hearing."

"This better be good." Why am I even letting him talk?

"Oh, it's good. Very good. Much better than you can even imagine." He strolls over to Harrier and slaps him in the face. "You still awake, Bird-brain? I'd hate for you to miss the most exciting part after three years of careful planning and moving everything into place."

Pierrot grabs Harrier by the chin and lifts his head up. Harrier winces.

"You think he's trying to clean up the city because criminals killed his father? That is what he told you, yes?" He lets go of Harrier's chin, and Harrier grits his teeth as he tries to hold his head up. After a second, his neck gives out again.

"Oh, no, no, no. You have it all wrong, boy. The Black Harrier is just trying to clean up the mess his daddy left behind. As this city's top criminal. You see, his papa's death left quite a vacuum at the top of the underworld. And we've all been trying to fill it ever since."

I look at Harrier to see if there's any reaction to help me figure out if Pierrot is telling the truth. He still can't lift his head.

"I don't care. Why should it matter to me *why* he does it? He's cleaning up the streets, getting rid of garbage like you."

"Why should it matter? Hmmm. Why *should* it matter?" He taps his index finger on his lip as if he's in deep thought, and turns back to Harrier. "What do you think, Frankie-boy? Should I tell him, or do you want to do the honors?"

With a huge effort, Harrier raises his head and looks Pierrot in the eye. His voice comes out as a rasp, but not the kind I usually make fun of. It almost sounds like a death rattle. "...no..."

"Fine. I'll do it then." Pierrot waddles over to me and gets right up in my face, and I have to do everything in my power not to punch him as hard as I can.

"The first reason you should care, young man, is that your mentor here was the one who killed him."

No. It can't be. That's our number one rule. Our only rule. *No killing.* How could Harrier have started his career by killing his own father?

"I know. Shocking, isn't it? But this squeaky clean do-gooder just couldn't handle the idea that his father was such a notorious blackguard, and it simply drove him over the edge. But wait...it gets better."

It makes me sick to see Pierrot relishing this so much. I'm not sure how much of my shaking is adrenaline, how much is due to my injuries and weakness, and how much is just from me wanting to thrash this evil bastard.

"The second reason—the most important reason—is that Franklin Douglas, Jr., kingpin of crime for many years, and responsible for more death, destruction, and misery than anyone else in this city's long history... was your granddaddy."

As my head tries to wrap itself around what Pierrot just said, I see a look of satisfaction come across his face like I've never witnessed from another person. It takes a second for me to register exactly what he means, but when it hits me, it hits me hard—like getting the wind knocked out of me.

And then Pierrot literally knocks the wind out of me. He hits me hard in the stomach, and I feel my diaphragm push all of the air out of my lungs. I lean forward and gasp for breath, and he hits me with an uppercut so hard that I feel myself standing up straight before falling back and hitting the ground.

Then he kicks me. First in the ribcage, then again in the kidneys. That's the first time I notice that he's wearing steel-toed shoes. I cough, and blood comes up.

I just want to lay here. To let him finish me off. It can't be true. But what if it is?

Pierrot looks down at me and I imagine that he's going to start laughing, but then I remember what Redhawk said about him not being that kind of clown. In fact, I don't remember him laughing at all during the two times we've interacted. He could kill me now, right in front of Harrier, but he's making sure what he revealed to me is sinking in.

My brain is trying to calculate how Harrier's dad could be my grandfather without it being the obvious answer. I met my mom's dad when I was little, before he died, so that can't be it. Could my dad have been Harrier's brother? No—he was definitely an only child.

That only leaves one other option. But it feels so wrong that my mind rebels against it. Pushes it out as if it's poison.

I turn to Harrier. "Is it true?"

No response.

"He's just saying it to get to me, right? To mess with my head." Harrier continues to hang from his chains, his head bowed low. I crawl over to him and get up close. Close enough that he can see me without lifting his head.

"Is. It. *True?*"

His response is barely a whisper. If it wasn't so quiet in here, I wouldn't have been able to hear it. "Yes."

I feel a new rage well up inside of me. One that I have to release. But I can't take it out on Harrier. Not right now. I spring from my position on the floor like a wild animal and land on Pierrot's rotund chest, knocking him to the ground. His head smacks against the floor.

I start pounding on his face with my fists. Even with all the violence I've witnessed and participated in, I've never seen anyone beaten as savagely as what I'm dishing out myself right now. It's like it's not even me—I feel like I'm watching everything happen on a TV show or in a video game. I don't even know how long it goes on for. My fists are covered in blood, and the makeup on Pierrot's face is now just a black, white, and red smear.

Through the rage and the hitting I somehow hear it. I don't know how many times he said it before I noticed, but it barely registers in my ears. Harrier's raspy, almost inaudible voice: "Stop."

I freeze, crouched on Pierrot's chest, my right fist raised high, ready to come down again. I'm breathing heavily and I can feel my heartbeat throbbing in my head. I look down at Pierrot's beaten, bloody face, barely clinging on to life. I watch as a drop of blood falls from my fist into the middle of Pierrot's forehead.

I look back at Harrier and see tears streaming down his face...the first time I've ever seen him cry.

Then Pierrot spits out some teeth and talks to me, his speech distorted by his broken nose and busted lips. "Do it."

And he laughs. For the first time, I hear the laugh of the sad clown, and it's more frightening than anything else he's done. Sick, twisted...evil.

And I suddenly realize why I'm really here. The truth about what's going on. Pierrot didn't lure me down here to kill me in front of Harrier. He'd already done that before with another Red Kite, and Harrier came back stronger than ever. He wanted me to kill *him* in front of Harrier. To break me. To get me to become the one thing Harrier and I could never live with: a murderer.

And it almost worked.

I roll off of Pierrot and look at his plump, broken face as he continues to laugh. At the very least, he has a concussion, a broken nose, and a dislocated jaw. Probably a detached retina. But he'll live if we get an ambulance here soon.

I manage to get myself up and stagger over to Harrier. Pulling my lock picks out again, I unlock the chains holding him and try to help him down to prevent him from dropping to the ground and injuring himself even more. I lower him to the floor, and he lies there momentarily, near unconsciousness. I need to call for an ambulance now that the building is secured. There's no way I can handle this myself at The Aerie.

Then Black Harrier does something more superhuman than anything I've ever known even Eaglestar to pull off, and pushes himself up to his hands and knees.

"You should relax, Harrier, we'll have help on the way soon." But he ignores me completely. "Frank, it's over."

Harrier starts to crawl over to Pierrot, who continues his insane fit of laughter. He reaches his nemesis and leans over him, barely able to hold himself up. If anything, Pierrot is laughing even harder now, gasping for breath.

Harrier grabs both sides of Pierrot's head. "Shut. Up." He twists Pierrot's head quickly and there's a sickening cracking sound.

And the laughter stops.

EPILOGUE

Dad.

Not a word I'm all that familiar with, especially when it comes to addressing someone. It's too weird for me to call Harrier that. At least for now.

Mr. Chen helped him create a story about how he was kidnapped and held for ransom for weeks. It explains his condition, as well as why Frank hasn't appeared in public for so long.

At first I didn't want to see him because I was so angry. I went to the hospital, but only to visit Osprey. She was in a wheelchair for a couple of weeks because of the fall, but she was healing quickly and back on her feet in no time.

I still never found out her name. One time when I went in to see her, she was asleep, and I tried to peek at her chart. But as soon as I reached for it, her eyes popped open, almost like she could sense it.

"Don't even think about it, buster." She had a half-smile, but I could tell she was serious about me not looking.

"Even after I saved your life?"

"You mean after I almost got killed helping *you* save your mentor?"

"Uh...yeah, well, if you put it that way..."

We both laughed, and I felt like we were really starting to connect. It actually seemed like she might even share more about herself soon, even if she wasn't ready yet that day.

Then, one day, I showed up to see her and she was gone. I guess I could probably find her somehow if I really wanted to. But if she wanted to see me, she wouldn't have left without telling me.

When I do finally see Harrier, I go easy on him at first, with how bad off he is physically and after all the psychological torture he must have endured. But after he's somewhat recovered, it's time for him to give me some answers. I visit him at his penthouse, where he's been healing from his injuries.

I start with the most important part. Why didn't he tell me I was his son? How could he keep that from me for three years? My whole life?

"I didn't know you existed until just before we met. Your mom and I met when we were young. I had no idea she was still in high school...she got into a club I own with a fake I.D. I never saw her again after our one night together, and she never contacted me about being pregnant. I get the impression she wasn't sur——-"

He cuts himself off, but I know what he's going to say. She wasn't sure who the father was, because he wasn't the only guy she had been with around that time. Knowing my mom, this isn't a surprise to me, and I'm long past it bothering me.

"So what changed?"

"A few years ago, I was contacted by a sleazy lawyer who claimed I had a child out there I wasn't aware of. Apparently, your mom had been seeing him, and mentioned that she had, uh, 'dated' me shortly before you were born."

He pauses and takes a long drink from his single-malt Scotch, his one other vice besides women.

"A man of my considerable means and...reputation is always slapped with paternity suits, most of which turn out to be false. The few that aren't, I...well, I make sure they're taken care of."

I can only hope he means financially, but now isn't the time to ask him to be more specific about that.

"This guy was different. He was ready to go to the papers, the news channels, the entire Internet. He didn't give a damn about me helping you or your mom; he was more interested in how much money he could get out of me if he kept quiet about it. As you can imagine, I don't appreciate being blackmailed."

I already feel sorry for this guy, who I vaguely remember my mom being with for a month or so, and Frank hasn't even told me what happened next.

"I had been on a...break from crime fighting, but it got me motivated again." I figure this must have been the time after the second Kite was killed. That would go along with what Redhawk told me.

"So Harrier paid him a visit. It didn't take much for me to uncover several things that would not only get him disbarred, but sent to prison, including jury tampering."

He smiles, and it kind of scares me because it isn't the fake Frank Douglas smile he uses in public. It's the smile the Black Harrier gets on the rare occasion when he enjoys his job.

"I also maybe...roughed him up a bit. Just enough to make sure he left Frank Douglas alone, as well as anyone else he was thinking about extorting. I also found out that your mom had no idea what he was doing."

I always wondered what happened to that guy. Not that my mom doesn't break up with guys often, but I do remember that relationship ending so abruptly that it puzzled her. "Didn't it matter to you that you might actually have a kid out there?"

"Of course it did. Just because I wouldn't allow that ambulance chaser to blackmail me doesn't mean I didn't want to make things right." He's so vehement about this that I have no doubt he's being honest.

"I immediately started investigating the situation. You, your mom, everything I could find. My plan was to get a hold of some of your DNA and test it against my own. But I didn't need to."

"Why?"

"Because one day you were attacked while I was observing you, and I saw you fight. You copied my moves exactly, and took out those thugs without much effort."

I think back to that first day we met. It's strange to hear about it from his point of view.

"Your ability is rare. Very few others have it, but I'm one of them. And I knew immediately you had inherited it from me. That's why I took you on as a protégé and began training you. So that you could use your ability properly and stay out of danger."

"But...how could you let me keep living in those crappy conditions when you knew I was your son?"

"Because I couldn't take you away from your mom, but I couldn't give her access to a lot of money either. I had Chen send a few checks from Douglas Industries at first——not much, but nothing to sneeze at, either——under the ruse that she was part of some class-action lawsuit against the company. I had to know how she would react." He takes another long drink.

"And...?"

"And she immediately blew it all on herself and her vices. From what I could tell, she didn't spend a cent on you or make any attempt to make your life better."

The look on my face must be pretty bad, because he looks like he doesn't want to go on.

"I'm sorry, I shouldn't—-"

"No. I want to know the truth. All of it." *No matter how much it hurts.*

"I was afraid that if she had even more money, she would end up overdosing or drinking herself to death. So instead, I tried to help you out directly as much as possible. Buying good food, electronic devices, letting you hang around here as often as possible."

So many things make more sense now. "Well, I'm glad I know now. When will you be able to return to crime fighting?"

"I won't."

The shock is so much, I almost feel the blow physically.

"I've been through too much. I'm getting too old. And I broke the rule we're never allowed to break. It's time for someone else to take over as The Black Harrier."

"Me?"

He smiles again, but this time it isn't scary or the fake one. "Someday. But you're not ready yet."

As if on cue, the false bookcase that serves as the entrance to The Aerie opens, and someone comes through dressed in the Harrier costume. He's still pulling on the gloves as he approaches us.

"Alex!" I stand up and run over to him. "How did you——? I thought you were——"

"Yeah, so did I. But I woke up on a fishing boat after some guys pulled me out of the water. I wasn't in as bad of shape as I should have been, but it still took me a little while to recover."

Frank struggles to stand and uses a cane to limp over to Alex. "How's it fit? I had it taken in somewhat."

"Not bad, but it's still a little loose in the stomach area." Frank gives Alex a look that tells me there's an in-joke there I'm not aware of.

Alex——Harrier——turns to me. "Well? Are you going to suit up or what? We have some patrolling to do."

"Let's go."

Alex turns to Frank again. "You sure you're ready to do this? No turning back?"

"You're The Black Harrier now."

"Good. Because I've made my first big decision already. I figure I'm going to need some extra help out there until I get up to your level, so I invited someone else to come along."

Osprey steps through the entrance and takes in the posh surroundings of the penthouse. "Nice crib."

Frank gets his old look back. "I thought I said——"

"Uh-uh-uh. I'm The Black Harrier now, and I get to choose my own sidekicks."

Osprey and I both respond at the exact same time. "*Partners.*"

"Oh. Right. Sorry." He heads for the entrance to The Aerie. "Well, then, let's go, *partners.*"

I'm definitely in the mood to beat up some bad guys.

SIDEKICK

ABOUT THE AUTHOR

Christopher J. Valin is a writer, artist, teacher and historian living in the Los Angeles area with his wife and two children. He has written stories of all kinds since childhood, including novels, short stories, comic books, and screenplays. In 2009, his biography of his 5x great-grandfather (based on his master's thesis in military history), *Fortune's Favorite: Sir Charles Douglas and the Breaking of the Line*, was published by Fireship Press.

In addition to writing and inking for independent comic book companies and writing screenplays for production companies, Christopher has had numerous short stories published in anthologies such as *Clockwork & Capes: Superheroes in the Age of Steam* and *Doomed: Tales of the Last Days*.

See more at **www.christophervalin.com**

Please leave a review at Amazon.com!

SIDEKICK

CHRISTOPHER J. VALIN